His heart ached with remembered pain. His body ached with un-fulfilled desire.

What was he doing? Why couldn't he just leave Eleanor Langley alone?

Ever since Eleanor had come back into his life—ever since he'd realised she was telling the truth—he hadn't been able to stop thinking of her. Thinking about the what-ifs, wondering if life could give them a second chance.

Jace stopped in his tracks. A second chance at what? At *love*?

Did he really want that?

The last ten years he'd been hardening his heart against love, against any messy emotion. He'd focused on his business, building an empire instead of a dynasty.

And yet now... Now he wanted more. He wanted Eleanor.

Ellie.

Kate Hewitt discovered her first Mills & Boon® romance on a trip to England when she was thirteen, and she's continued to read them ever since. She wrote her first story at the age of five, simply because her older brother had written one and she thought she could do it too. That story was one sentence long—fortunately they've become a bit more detailed as she's grown older. She has written plays, short stories, and magazine serials for many years, but writing romance remains her first love. Besides writing, she enjoys reading, travelling, and learning to knit.

After marrying the man of her dreams—her older brother's childhood friend—she lived in England for six years, and now resides in Connecticut with her husband, her three young children, and the possibility of one day getting a dog. Kate loves to hear from readers—you can contact her through her website: www.kate-hewitt.com

BOUND TO
THE GREEK

BY
KATE HEWITT

All the characters in this book have no existence outside the imagination of the author, and have no relation whatsoever to anyone bearing the same name or names. They are not even distantly inspired by any individual known or unknown to the author, and all the incidents are pure invention.

First published in Great Britain 2011
Harlequin Mills & Boon Limited,
Eton House, 18-24 Paradise Road, Richmond, Surrey TW9 1SR

© Kate Hewitt 2011

ISBN: 978 0 263 88623 8

Harlequin Mills & Boon policy is to use papers that are natural, renewable and recyclable products and made from wood grown in sustainable forests. The logging and manufacturing process conform to the legal environmental regulations of the country of origin.

Printed and bound in Spain
by Litografia Rosés, S.A., Barcelona

BOUND TO
THE GREEK

To all the lost little ones, including mine.

CHAPTER ONE

'COME right this way, Mr Zervas. You're going to meet with Eleanor, our top planner.'

Jace Zervas stilled his stride for no more than a second as the word reverberated through him. *Eleanor*. He hadn't heard that name in ten years, hadn't let himself think it.

Of course, it had to be a coincidence. There were certainly more Eleanors in the United States—in New York City—than the one who had broken his heart.

The assistant who had led him through the elegantly sparse lobby with its designer sofas and modern art now stopped in front of a door of tinted glass, gave a perfunctory knock, then pushed it open.

'Eleanor? I'd like to introduce you to—'

Jace didn't hear the rest. For as the woman in the office swung round to face him, his mind buzzed, blanked. It *was* Eleanor.

His Eleanor. Ellie.

He knew she was as surprised as he was that he was here, that *they* were here, face to face. Although her expression didn't really change, he was aware of the slight widening of her eyes, the parting of her lips.

Then she drew herself up, gave him a professional smile that managed to irritate him with its coolness, and said, 'Thank you, Jill. That will be all.'

The assistant, surely aware of the current that crackled through the air, glanced speculatively between them. Jace ignored her, his gaze fixed on Eleanor Langley, so utterly, appallingly different from the Ellie he'd once known. 'Shall I bring coffee?'

A tiny pause. 'Certainly. Thank you.'

The assistant left, the door clicked shut, and Jace's mind kicked back into gear.

Of course he should have expected this might happen. He'd known Ellie was from New York, and her mother was an event planner. Why shouldn't she have followed the same career path?

Because the Ellie you knew hated her mother's career, her mother's world. The Ellie you knew—or at least thought you knew—wanted to open a bakery.

Clearly much had happened in the last ten years.

'You've changed.' He didn't mean to say it, yet it was impossible not to notice it. The Ellie he'd known ten years ago had looked nothing like the shiny, polished woman in front of him.

His Ellie had been relaxed, natural, *fun*, so different from this woman with her tailored black power suit, her high-lighted hair barely brushing her cheekbones in an elegant chestnut bob. Her hazel eyes, once warm and golden, now seemed darker, sharper, and were narrowed into assessing slits. As she moved back around to her desk Jace saw her shoes: black three-inch stilettos. His Ellie had never worn heels. His Ellie had never worn black.

Yet why was he even thinking this way? *His* Ellie hadn't been his at all. He'd realised that all too terribly when he'd last seen her…when she'd lied to him in the worst way possible. When he'd walked away without another word.

Eleanor Langley stared down at the burnished surface of her desk and took a deep breath. She needed the moment to regain her poise and control. She'd never expected this moment to happen, although she'd fantasised about it many times over the last decade. Coming face to face with Jace

Zervas. Telling him just what she thought of him and his cowardly creeping away.

She'd envisioned herself slapping his face, telling him to go to hell, or, in her more dignified moments, sweeping him with one simple, disdainful glance.

She had not pictured herself trembling, both inside and out, unable to think of a single thing to say.

Stop. She'd worked too hard for too long to let this moment defeat her. Taking another breath, Eleanor lifted her head and settled her gaze coolly on the man in front of her.

'Of course I've changed. It's been ten years.' She paused, letting her gaze sweep over him, although she had a feeling it wasn't as disdainful as she might have wished. 'You've changed too, Jace.' It felt strange to have his name on her lips. She never spoke of him. She tried not to think of him.

He *had* changed; his ink-black hair was now streaked with grey at the temples and his face looked leaner, longer. Harder. Eleanor noticed new lines from nose to mouth, and the faint fanning of crow's feet by his eyes. Somehow those lines didn't age him so much as give him an air of dignity and experience. They even emphasised the steely grey of his eyes with their silvery glints. And his body hadn't changed at all, it seemed: still long, lithe, and powerful. The grey silk suit he wore only emphasised his muscular shoulders and trim hips; he wore it, as he had the cashmere sweatshirts and faded jeans of his college days, with ease and grace.

He looked, she thought a bit resentfully, great. But then, she reminded herself, so did she. She spent a lot of time and effort making sure she looked great; in her job a professional and even glamorous appearance was a must. She was grateful for it now. The last thing she wanted was to be at a disadvantage. She straightened, smiled even, and flicked her hair back from her face in one quick movement. 'So you're my two o'clock.'

Jace smiled back, faintly, but his eyes were hard. He looked almost angry. Eleanor had no idea what *he* had to be angry about; he was the one who had left. If anyone should be angry— She stopped that thought before her resentful mind gave it wings. She wasn't angry. She was over it. Over him. She no longer cared any more, at all, about Jace Zervas.

She turned to her planner, still open on her desk, and trailed one glossily manicured finger down the day's appointments. 'You're here on behalf of Atrikides Holdings?' she asked. 'It says Leandro Atrikides was supposed to have been coming.' She looked up, eyebrows arched. 'Change of plans?'

'Something like that,' Jace agreed, his voice taut. He sat down in one of the leather armchairs in front of her desk and crossed one leg over the other.

'Well.' She made herself smile and sat down behind her desk, hands neatly folded. 'How can I help?'

Jace's lips tightened, and Eleanor wondered if that was going to be it. Ten years of anger, bitterness, and overwhelming heartache reduced to nothing in a single sentence. *How can I help?* Yet what other choice was there? She didn't want to rake over the past; it would be messy and uncomfortable and far too painful. She wanted to pretend the past didn't exist, and so she would. She'd treat Jace Zervas like a regular client, even though he was far from one, and she hardly wanted to help him. She didn't even want to talk to the man for another second.

The sane thing, of course, would be to respectfully request a colleague to take Jace as her client, and step away from what could only be an explosive situation. Or if not explosive, then at least angrily simmering. She could see it in the hard steel of his eyes. She could feel it bubbling in herself.

Yet Eleanor knew she wouldn't do that. Her boss wouldn't be pleased; Lily Stevens didn't like changes. Messes. And Eleanor could certainly do without the gossip. Besides, there was another, greater reason why she'd face Jace down in her own office. She didn't want to give him the satisfaction of making her run away. As he had.

'Well,' Jace replied after a moment, 'obviously I'm here because I need you to plan an event.'

'Obviously,' Eleanor agreed, and heard the answering sharpness in her tone. This was not going well. Every little exchange was going to be pointed under the politeness, and she didn't think she could take the tension. The trouble was, she didn't know what else to do. Talking about the past was akin to ripping the bandages off old wounds, inflaming the scars that still remained on her heart. Her body. Even re-membering it hurt.

She clamped her mind down on that thought. Jace Zervas was just another client, she told herself again. Just a regular client. She let her breath out slowly and tried to smile.

'What I meant,' she said evenly, 'was what kind of event are you hosting?' She gritted her teeth as she added, 'Some details would help.'

'Isn't there some form that's been filled out? I'm quite sure my assistant did this all on the telephone.'

Eleanor glanced through the slim file she had on Atrikides Holdings. 'A Christmas party,' she read from the memo one of the secretaries had taken. 'That's all I have, I'm afraid.'

A knock sounded on the door, and Jill came in with a tray of coffee. Eleanor rose to take it from her. She didn't want her assistant picking up on the tension that thrummed angrily through the room. God knew how she'd try to use it; Jill had been jockeying for her position since she arrived, fresh from college, two years ago.

'Thanks, Jill. I'll take it from here.'

Surprised, Jill backed off, the door closing once more, and Eleanor set the tray on her desk, her back to Jace. She still heard his lazy murmur.

'You didn't used to drink coffee. I always thought it was so funny, a girl who wanted to open a coffee shop and yet didn't drink coffee herself.'

Eleanor tensed. So he was going to go there. She'd been hoping they could get through this awkward meeting without referencing the past at all, but now Jace was going to talk about these silly, student memories, as if they shared some happy past.

As if they shared anything at all.

A single streak of anger, white-hot, blazed through her. Her hands shook as she poured the coffee. How dared he? How dared he act as if he hadn't walked—run—away from her, the minute things got too much? How dared he pretend they'd parted amicably, or even parted at all?

Instead of her going to his apartment building, only to find he'd left. Left the building, left the city, left the country. All without telling her.

Coward.

'Actually, I think it was enterprising,' she told him coolly, her back still to him. Her hands no longer trembled. 'I saw the market, and I wanted to meet it.' She handed him his coffee: black, two sugars, the way he'd always taken it. She still remembered. Still remembered brewing him a single-serve cafétière in her student apartment while she plied him with the pastries and cakes she was going to sell in her little bakery. While she told him her dreams.

He'd said everything was delicious. But of course he would. He'd lied about so many things, like when he'd said he loved her. If he'd loved her, he wouldn't have left.

Eleanor poured her own coffee. She took it black now, and drank at least three cups a day. Her best friend Allie said so much caffeine wasn't good for her, but Eleanor needed the kick. Especially now.

She turned back to Jace. He still held his mug, his long, brown fingers wrapped around the handle, his expression brooding and a little dark. 'That's not how I remember it.'

Disconcerted, Eleanor took too large a sip of coffee and burned her tongue. 'What?'

Jace leaned forward. 'You weren't interested in meeting a market. You weren't even interested in business. Don't you remember, Ellie?' His voice came out in a soft hiss. 'You just wanted to have a place where people could relax and be happy.' He spoke it like a sneer, and Eleanor could only think of when—and where—she had said that. In Jace's bed, after they'd made love for the first time. She'd shared so many pitiful, pathetic secrets with him. Poured out her life and heart and every schoolgirl dream she'd ever cherished, and he'd given her—what? Nothing. Less than nothing.

'I'm sure we remember quite a few things differently, Jace,' she said coolly. 'And I go by Eleanor now.'

'You told me you hated your name.'

She let out an impatient breath. 'It's been ten years, Jace. Ten years. I've changed. You've changed. Get over it.'

His eyes narrowed, the colour flaring to silver. 'Oh, I'm over it, Eleanor,' he said softly. 'I'm definitely over it.'

But he didn't sound over it. He sounded angry, and that made Eleanor even angrier despite all her intentions to stay cool, not to care. He had no right, no right at all, even to be the tiniest bit furious. Yet here he was, acting as if she'd been the one to do something wrong. Of course she *had* done something wrong, in Jace's eyes. She'd made the classic, naive mistake of accidentally getting pregnant.

Jace stared at her, felt the fury rise up in him before he choked it all down again. There was no use in being angry. It was ten years too late. He didn't want to feel angry; the emotion shamed him now.

Yet even so he realised he wanted to know. He needed to know what had happened to Eleanor in the last ten years. Had she kept the baby? Had she married the father? Had she suffered even a moment's regret for trying to dupe him so damnably? Because she didn't look as if she had. She looked as if she was angry with him, which was ridiculous. She was the guilty one, the lying one. He'd simply found out.

'So.' She sat down again, behind the desk, so it served as a barrier between them. Not that they needed one. Time was enough. Putting her coffee carefully to one side, she pulled out a pen and pad of paper. Jace watched the way her hair swung down in a smooth, dark curtain as she bent her head. Everything about her was so different from the Ellie he had known, the Ellie he remembered. The woman in front of him was no more than a polished, empty shell. She gave nothing away. She looked up, her hazel eyes narrowing, her mouth curving into a false smile. 'Can you give me a few details about this party?'

Damn the party. Jace leaned forward. 'Did you have a boy or a girl?' God only knew why he wanted to ask that question. Why he even wanted to know. Surely there were a dozen—a hundred—more relevant questions he could have asked. *When did you cheat on me? Why? Who was he? Did he love you like I did?*

No, he wasn't about to ask any of those questions. They all revealed too much. He had no intention of letting Eleanor Langley ever know how much she'd hurt him.

His voice was no more than a predatory hiss, an accusation, yet Ellie's expression didn't change. If anything it became even more closed, more polished and professional. The woman was like ice. He could hardly credit it; the Ellie he'd known had reflected every emotion in her eyes. She'd cried at commercials. Now Ellie—Eleanor—simply pressed her lips together and gave her head a little shake.

'Let's not talk about the past, Jace. If we want to be professional—' Her voice caught, finally, and he was glad. He'd almost thought she didn't feel anything and God knew he felt too much. So this icy woman could thaw. A little. Underneath there was something, something true and maybe even broken, something *real*, and for now that was enough.

He leaned back, satisfied. 'Fine. Let's be professional. I want to hold a Christmas party for the remaining employees of Atrikides Holdings.'

'Remaining?' Ellie repeated a bit warily.

'Yes, remaining. I bought the company last week, and there has been some unrest because of it.'

'A corporate takeover.' She spoke the words distastefully.

'Yes, exactly,' Jace replied blandly. 'I had to let some of the employees go when I brought in my own people. Now that there is a new workforce, I'd like to create a feeling of goodwill. A Christmas party is a means to that end.'

'I see.'

Yet Jace could see from the flicker of contempt in her eyes, the tightening of her mouth, that she didn't see at all. She was summing him up and judging him up based on very little evidence—the evidence he'd given.

Yet why should he care what she thought of him? And why should she judge at all? She'd been just as ruthless as he was, as enterprising and economical with the truth.

And he'd judged her with far more damning information.

Eleanor wrote a few cursory notes on the pad of paper on her desk. She wasn't even aware of what she was writing. Her vision hazed, her mind blanked.

Was it a boy or a girl?

How could he ask such a question now, with such contempt? His *child*. He'd been asking about his child.

She closed her mind on the thought like a trap, refusing to free the memory and sorrow. She couldn't go there. Not now, not ever. She'd kept those emotions locked deep inside herself and even seeing Jace Zervas again wouldn't free them. She wouldn't let it. She drew in a deep breath and looked up.

'So what kind of Christmas party are we talking about here? Cocktails, sit-down dinner? How many people do you anticipate coming?'

'There are only about fifty employees, and I'd like to invite families.' Jace spoke tonelessly. 'Quite a few have small children, so something family-friendly but elegant.'

'Family-friendly,' Eleanor repeated woodenly. She felt her fingers clench around the pen she was holding. She could not do this. She could not pretend a moment longer, even though she'd been pretending for ten years—

Was that all her life had been? Pretending? Pretence? And she hadn't realised it until she'd come face to face with Jace Zervas.

Stop, she told herself yet again. *Stop thinking, feeling.*

Another breath. Somehow she made herself nod as she wrote another note on the pad of paper. 'Very well. Now—'

'Look,' Jace exhaled impatiently, 'I don't really have time to go over every detail. I came here as a favour, and I have a lot to do. I'm only in New York for a week.'

'A week—'

'I need the party to be this Friday,' Jace cut her off.

Eleanor's mouth dropped open before she quickly closed it. *That* hadn't been on the memo. 'I'm afraid that's impossible. Venues are booked, I have a complete client list—'

'Nothing is impossible if you throw enough money at it,' Jace replied flatly. 'And I chose your company because I was assured you could make it happen.' His gaze, cold and contemptuous, raked over her. 'I was told the top event planner would see to me personally. I suppose that's you?'

Eleanor merely nodded. She didn't trust herself to speak.

'Then email me a list of details to go over by tomorrow morning.' Jace rose from his chair. 'You've done very well for yourself, Ellie,' he said softly. 'I wonder how many people you had to climb over to get to this lovely little spot.' He glanced out of the window at her view of Madison Square Park, the leafless trees stark against a grey winter sky.

His comment was so blatantly unfair and unwarranted that Eleanor could only gasp. And fume. What right did he have to make such a judgment? If anyone should be *judging*—

Jace headed for the door. 'I don't think I'll need to see you before the party,' he said, and somehow this bored dismissal stung her more than anything else had.

He was going to leave, just like that, after raking up the old wounds, after asking about her baby—their baby—

'It was a girl,' she burst out, the words like staccato gunfire. Her chest burned, and so did her eyes. Her fingers clenched into a fist on her desk. Jace stilled, his hand on the door. 'A girl,' she repeated tonelessly. 'Since you asked.'

He turned around slowly, lip curled in an unpleasant sneer. 'So I did,' he replied. 'But actually I really don't care.'

And then he was gone.

CHAPTER TWO

'ELEANOR? Did Jace Zervas just leave the office?'

Eleanor jerked her head up to see her boss, Lily Stevens, standing in her office doorway. Under her glossy black helmet of hair her eyebrows were drawn together sharply, her mouth a thin red line. The elegantly disapproving look reminded Eleanor of her mother, which was unsurprising since Lily and her mother had been business partners until five years ago.

'Eleanor?' Lily repeated, more sharply, and Eleanor rose from her desk, trying to smile. How long had she been lost in her own miserable reverie? 'Yes. We just concluded our meeting.'

'That was fast.'

Eleanor moved around her desk to put Jace's coffee cup—barely touched—back on the tray. 'He's a busy man.'

'Jill said things seemed tense when she came in here.'

Of course Jill would run to her boss, Eleanor thought with resentment. What a frenemy! This business could be cut-throat, and everyone was trying to claw a way in or up. She gave a little shrug. 'Not really.'

'I don't think I need to tell you,' Lily said, her tone making it clear she thought she did, 'that Jace Zervas is a very important client? His holdings are worth over a billion—'

'You don't need to tell me.' She didn't need Lily telling her how rich and powerful Jace was. She'd known that already. When she'd met him as a twenty-two-year-old exchange student in Boston, he'd been from money. Rich, entitled, spoiled.

Except he'd never seemed spoiled to her…until he'd left. Then he'd seemed rotten right through.

'I want you to do everything in your power to make this party a success,' Lily told her. 'I'm releasing your other clients to Laura for the week.'

'What?' Eleanor heard the outrage in her voice, and strove to temper it. She had several clients she'd been working with for months, and she knew Laura—another frenemy—would be eager to scoop up the contacts and run with them. Eleanor gritted her teeth. This business could be brutal. She'd toughened up a lot in the last ten years, but it still made her weary. She also knew there was nothing she could do about it.

If Lily was going to make that kind of executive decision, so be it. He wasn't worth her jeopardising her career; he wasn't worth *anything*. She would work on Jace's damn party for a week. And then she would forget—again—that she'd ever met him.

Lily's eyes narrowed. 'Is that going to be a problem, Eleanor?'

Eleanor bit the inside of her cheek. She hated that tone, that silky, dangerous, warning tone that her mother had always taken with her as a child. Funny, how she'd ended up in a job just like her mother's, with a boss just like her mother.

Except there was nothing remotely funny about it, or even coincidental. Every choice, every decision had been intentional, a way of distancing herself from everything she'd been or believed in. A way of reinventing herself.

And it had worked.

Now she turned to smile sweetly at her boss. 'Of course not. I'm absolutely thrilled—and honoured, Lily—to be working with Mr Zervas. Getting his account is a coup for the agency.'

Lily nodded, seemingly satisfied. 'So it is. Are you meeting with Zervas again?'

'I'll email him the particulars tomorrow.' Eleanor shuddered inwardly to think what that meant. She'd be tied up in begging calls for the rest of the day, recalling favours and currying some more so she could make this thing happen.

The idea that she would have to slave away all for Jace burned in her gut, her heart. It was just *wrong*.

But she wasn't about to lose her job over this, or even her cool. And, Eleanor told herself, there could be some sweet, sweet satisfaction in showing Jace how he hadn't hurt her at all.

Even if he really had—and horribly at that.

She spent the rest of the day immersed in work, planning Jace's party while refusing to think of the man himself. A call to Atrikides Holdings yielded some interesting—and unsurprising—information.

'It all happened so fast,' gushed the staff member Eleanor had been connected to when she asked to speak to someone about details. Eleanor leaned back in her chair and prepared to hear some gossip. 'One minute everything was fine—it's a family business, you know—and the next he swooped in and took over. Fired half the people.' The woman—Peggy—lowered her voice to an awed hush. 'They had to leave that very day. Pack their stuff in boxes. Even Talos Atrikides—the CEO's *son*!'

'Well, hopefully this party will go some way to smoothing things over,' Eleanor replied. She could listen to the gossip, but she wouldn't indulge in it herself. She knew better.

Still, as she hung up the phone, the conversation left her a little shaken. She'd fallen in love with Jace Zervas when he'd been just twenty-two years old, charming, easy-going, carefree and careless. She hadn't realised just how cold—and cold-hearted—he'd been until he'd walked away.

And hearing about his actions with Atrikides Holdings today confirmed it. He really was that man.

The other one—the one she'd fallen in love with—had been nothing more than a mirage. A lie.

It was nearly midnight by the time Eleanor finally

stumbled out of the office, exhausted and eyesore from scanning endless sheets of paper with their myriad details. Still, she had the basis of a party to propose to Jace—via email—tomorrow. Massaging her temples, she headed out into the street, the only cars visible a few off-duty cabs. It looked as if she would have to walk.

It was only a few blocks to her apartment in a high-rise condo on the Hudson River, a gleaming testament to glass and steel. Eleanor didn't particularly like the modern architecture, or the building's fussy, high-maintenance residents, but she'd bought it because her mother had said it was a good investment. And she didn't spend much time there anyway.

Sighing, Eleanor nodded hello to the doorman on duty and then headed in the high-speed lift up to the thirtieth floor.

Her apartment was, as always, dark and quiet. Eleanor dropped her keys on the hall table and flicked on the recessed lighting that bathed the living room with its modern sofa and teakwood coffee table in soft yellow light. Outside the Hudson River twinkled with lights.

Her stomach rumbled and she realised she had skipped dinner. Again. Kicking off her heels, she went to the galley kitchen and peered in her near-empty fridge. It held half a carton of moo shoo pork and a yogurt that was—Eleanor peered closer—two weeks past its sell-by date. Neither looked appetising.

Dispiritedly Eleanor closed the fridge. It was hard to believe she'd once baked cookies and muffins by the dozen, had dreamed of owning her own café. She'd been unbearably, determinedly domestic, and now she could barely feed herself.

She grabbed a handful of rather stale crackers from the cupboard and went back to the living room. Funny, she hadn't thought of her old café dream in years, yet when she'd known Jace she'd spent hours embroidering that daydream, how it would be a little bit of everything: coffee shop, bakery, bookstore, gallery. Warm, cosy, bright, and welcoming. The home she'd never felt she'd had. It—everything—had seemed so possible then, so bright and shiny.

And now having Jace back in her life so suddenly, so surprisingly, brought it all back. The dreams, the disappointments.

The despair.

Eleanor thrust the thought away as she munched another cracker. Her stomach rumbled again. Perhaps sleep was better. She was exhausted anyway, and at least when she was asleep she wouldn't feel hungry. Neither would she have to think—or remember.

Dropping her uneaten crackers in the bin, Eleanor turned towards her bedroom.

Yet as she lay in the darkness of her room, the duvet pulled up to her chest, sleep didn't come. She was exhausted yet her eyes were wide open and gritty. And despite her best effort for them not to, the memories came, slipping into her mind, winding around her heart.

Lying there in the dark, she could almost feel the late autumn sunshine slanting onto the wide-planked wooden floors of her college apartment. She saw herself, tousle-haired, young, laughing, holding out a cupcake to Jace. They weren't lovers then; they hadn't even kissed. Yet. He'd invited himself over to taste the treats she'd been telling him about when he'd come into the café where she worked for his morning latte. And high with anticipation, Eleanor had invited him in, revelling in the charged atmosphere as he took a bite of the cupcake right from her hand, and then, laughing, pulled her close for a kiss.

It had been so easy, so right, and she'd gone without even considering another option, a different choice. He'd tasted like chocolate.

She closed her eyes, her throat tight and aching. She didn't want to resurrect these memories. She worked hard never to remember them. Yet they came anyway, so sweet and yet so bitter for what came afterward.

The empty apartment. The disconnected cellphone. The

bounced emails. The cold, cold despair when she'd realised just how alone she was.

Groaning alone, Eleanor turned on her side, tucking her knees up to her chest, and clenched her eyes shut as if that could keep the memories from coming and consuming her.

The blip of her baby on the monitor. The hard, sharp edge of the examining table, the cold slime of the gel on her tummy, and the endless silence of the technician, frowning, as she stared at the scan.

What's wrong?

Eleanor bolted up in bed and went to the bathroom for a herbal sleeping pill. She might have faced down Jace today, but she couldn't face the memories at night. They tormented her in a way even he never had. Their stark truth remained lodged in her gut, in her heart, like a stone. Nothing would remove it, or take away the bleak knowledge that she could never—

Eleanor closed her eyes again, tightly, and to her relief she finally slipped into a sleep made sweet by its absence of memories or dreams.

Despite her bad night, Eleanor was at her desk by eight o'clock in the morning. She saw Lily walk past her office door, nodding grimly, and she knew she'd been right to hurry to her desk that morning. She'd email the party plans to Jace, and then she'd put him out of her mind for ever. Or at least until he emailed back.

It took her nearly an hour to compose the email; it was aggravatingly difficult to strike the right tone, professional yet personable. She didn't want Jace to think for a second that she was affected by him. That she'd been hurt. Yet she hardly wanted to seem too friendly, either; that smacked of desperation.

Too tired to tweak the email any more, Eleanor just ended up sending a rather boring list of details, explaining in dry terms the choice of venue, the seating plan, the floral arrangements, the menu.

Then she determinedly pressed send.

Two minutes later her phone rang.

'This is completely unacceptable.'

Dumbly Eleanor stared at her computer screen, with its 'your message has been sent' confirmation still visible. It seemed impossible that in the approximately one hundred and twenty seconds since she'd pressed send, Jace had read her entire email and deemed it all unsuitable. Unacceptable, even.

'Excuse me?'

Over the phone Eleanor heard Jace exhale impatiently. 'This is all very standard, Ellie—'

'Don't call me that,' she said sharply. He ignored her.

'If I wanted a run-of-the-mill upscale do, I could have gone elsewhere. I came to Premier Planning because I was told you'd give me something extraordinary.'

Eleanor closed her eyes and prayed for patience. For mercy. She counted to ten, all the while listening to Jace's impatience, hearing it in those short little exhalations of breath, and then said coolly, 'I assure you there will be nothing run-of-the-mill about this party.'

Jace made a sound of disbelief that came close to a snort. 'Salmon pâté? Gardenias? Champagne? Standard luxuries.'

'That's an oxymoron, if ever I've heard one—'

'All of it is run-of-the-mill, Ellie.'

'I told you, don't call me that,' she snapped.

'Then impress me.'

That was the last thing she wanted to do. Why would she want to impress the man who had treated her like dirt, who had ground her heart into dust? Was her job really worth that much, worth her own dignity and pride?

Of course it was. It had to be. For the last ten years her job had been just about the only thing she had valued, the one thing she'd poured herself into. She wasn't risking it for Jace. He'd already done enough damage in her life.

'You gave me less than twenty-four hours to come up with

an entire event,' she finally ground out. 'Of course I haven't worked out all the details yet—'

'I expected better than this.'

'Funny, I said that ten years ago,' Eleanor snapped. Then she closed her eyes. The last, the very last thing she wanted was to drag the past—their past—into this mess. And from the taut silence crackling along the phone lines, she had a feeling Jace felt the same.

'You have no idea,' he said coldly. 'Meet me at my office building for lunch, twelve o'clock sharp.' And then he hung up.

Eleanor cursed aloud, just as Lily poked her head in her office door and smiled narrowly.

'Everything all right, Eleanor?'

'Fine,' Eleanor replied thinly. 'I just got a paper cut, that's all.'

Jace hung up the phone, massaging his knuckles as if he'd been in a fight. That terse conversation had not been a satisfactory outlet for his anger, for from the moment he'd walked into Eleanor Langley's office and seen her cool little smile that was what he'd been feeling. *Rage*.

He was furious that she seemed so unrepentant, that she'd attempted to foist another man's baby on him and didn't even possess the decency now to admit it or apologise. Yet what had he really expected of a woman who was willing to sink so low, to lie to someone she'd said she loved?

He didn't want to feel so angry, hated how it made the control he'd guarded carefully these last ten years slip away, so he hardly even knew what he was going to say or do. Or feel.

He'd never expected to feel so angry. He'd thought he'd got over Eleanor Langley and her betrayal, had put it far, far behind him. Now it felt fresh and raw and that made him even angrier. He didn't want Eleanor to affect him this much. He didn't want her to affect him at all.

Sighing impatiently, Jace turned back to the papers on his

desk. Atrikides Holdings was a mess and he had plenty to occupy both his mind and his time. He didn't need to waste either on Eleanor Langley, not even for a second.

All he wanted from her was a party. That was the only reason he was inviting her to lunch, why he was even bothering to see her again. He'd make it clear just what kind of high standard of service he expected. He'd put her in her place. His lips curved in a humourless smile as his sense of calm return to cloak him in reassuring coldness. All he wanted from her was a party, and by God he'd get one.

Three hours later Eleanor stood in front of the dark gleaming skyscraper that housed the offices of Atrikides Holdings. She took a deep breath and let it out slowly, and then resolutely headed for the door.

After she was cleared through security she took the lift to the building's top floor and stepped out into a room of elegant, old-style luxury with a stunning view of Central Park. She stared at the yawning rectangle of green, surrounded by concrete, the trees stark and bare above, as the elderly assistant pursed her lips before pressing a button on her telephone.

'Mr Zervas, I have Eleanor Langley for you.'

The reply was sharp, terse. 'Send her in.'

'You may go in,' the assistant said, nodding towards the wood-panelled double doors at the far end of the room.

Eleanor nodded back, swallowing down the sudden flutter of nerves that had risen to flurry wildly in her throat. She hated that she was nervous, almost as if Jace scared her. She would not let herself be cowed by him, not when he had been in the wrong ten years ago, not when *he* had been the coward then.

She certainly wouldn't be the coward now.

Squaring her shoulders, she knocked once, perfunctorily, before opening the doors and striding into the room.

The office was elegant, huge, and clearly not his. In one quick glance Eleanor saw the portraits of several Atrikides men on the walls, a side table cluttered with family photos. Children. She averted her eyes from the pictures. This had to be the office of the former CEO of Atrikides Holdings, Eleanor surmised, whom Jace had ousted along with half of the company's employees. A cold-blooded, corporate take-over. Should it really surprise her at all?

Jace stood behind the desk, his back to her. He didn't turn around even though he must have heard her come in.

Faintly annoyed, Eleanor cleared her throat. He turned, and in that moment—a single second, no more—her breath dried and her heart beat fast and she remembered how good it had been between them, how she'd lain in his arms as the sun washed them in gold and he'd kissed her closed eyelids.

She forced the memory—so sweet and painful—away and smiled coolly. 'You've taken over the CEO's office, I see.'

Jace waved a hand in dismissal. 'For the time being. It's convenient.'

'And he was fired along with most of the employees, I suppose?'

'Most is an exaggeration,' Jace replied, his eyes narrowing, flashing steel.

Eleanor wondered why she was asking. It was almost as if she was trying to pick a fight—and perhaps she was, for the anger and resentment still simmered beneath her surface, threatening to bubble forth. She wanted to hurt him, and yet she knew she wouldn't succeed with these silly little jabs. She'd only hurt herself, by revealing her own vulnerability. The fact that she was making them at all spoke of how hurt she had been and still was. She drew in a steadying breath and managed a small smile. 'You'd like to talk about the plans?'

Jace didn't smile back. 'I'm not sure they're worth discussing.'

Eleanor bit the inside of her cheek. 'Fine,' she said when she could be sure her voice was level, 'let's discard them if you find them so unsuitable. But you could at least make an effort to be civil.'

To her surprise, Jace acknowledged the point with one terse nod. 'Very well. Let's have lunch.'

He led her to a table hidden in the alcove, a tiny little table set intimately for two. Eleanor swallowed hard. She didn't know if she could do this. Every second she spent with Jace strained the composure she'd been working at maintaining for the last ten years, the air of professionalism that had become her armour. Just one sardonic look from those steely eyes—she remembered when they'd softened in pleasure, in love—made her calm façade crack. It crumbled, and she was defenceless once more, the cracks in her armour letting in the memories and pain.

She hated that she was so weak.

Jace drew her chair for her, the epitome of politeness, and with a murmured thanks Eleanor sat down. Her hands trembled as she placed her napkin in her lap. Jace sat in the chair opposite, his fingers steepled under his chin, his dark eyebrows drawn together. He looked so much the same, Eleanor thought with a lurch of remembered feeling, and yet so different. His hair was cut closer now, sprinkled with grey, and his skin looked more weathered. That glint of laughter in his eyes was gone, vanished completely. Yet he still possessed the same compelling aura, like a magnetic field around him. He still drew her to him, even though she hated the thought. Even now she could feel her body's traitorous reaction to his—the shaft of pleasure deep in her belly, the tingle of awareness as he reached for his own napkin, his fingers scant inches from hers. Eleanor made herself look away and a staff member came in to serve them.

'Would you care for a glass of wine?' Jace asked.

'I don't normally—'

'Half, then.' He held up the bottle, one eyebrow arched in silent challenge, poised to pour. Jerkily Eleanor nodded. This felt like a battle of wills, a contest over who could be the most professional. And she'd win. She *had* to. If he was so unaffected, well, then, she could be too, or at least seem as if she were. *Pretend.*

She could pretend to Jace and perhaps even to herself that the room didn't seethe with memories, that her heart wasn't splintering along its sewn-up seams. She *could*. It was the only way of getting out of here alive.

'Thank you.' She stared down at her salad, the leaves arranged artfully on a porcelain plate with an elegant little drizzle of vinaigrette. She had no appetite at all. Finally she stabbed a lettuce leaf with her fork and looked up. 'So why don't you tell me what kind of party you'd prefer?' She strove to keep her voice reasonable. 'If I have a few more details, we can brainstorm some ideas—'

'I thought that was your job. I already gave you a list of requirements—'

'You gave me less than twenty-four hours to mock up a plan,' Eleanor returned, her voice edged with anger, 'and a week to put it all together. Those are impossible conditions.'

Jace smiled thinly, his voice smooth and yet still conveying contempt. 'Your boss assured me your company was up to the task.'

Eleanor looked away and silently counted to ten. Breathe. In. Out. In. Out. 'I assure you, I am up to the task. But since the original plans were so unsatisfactory, perhaps I need a little more information about what you're looking for.' She hated this, hated feeling as if she had to kowtow to Jace, hated knowing he was baiting her simply because he could. At this moment it was hard to believe that they'd ever felt anything for each other but bitterness and dislike.

Jace exhaled impatiently. 'I want something unique and elegant, that shows the employees of this company that they will be cared for.'

'Except for the ones who were fired, you mean,' Eleanor retorted, then wished she could have held her tongue. Why was she so hung up on that? Who cared how Jace did business? She certainly couldn't afford to.

He arched one eyebrow, coldly disdainful. 'Are you questioning my business practices?'

'No, I just object to the idea of a party that makes it look like you care about these people when you really don't.' Jace stilled, his face blanking, and too late Eleanor realised how she had betrayed herself. Who she'd really been talking about.

Me.

She let out a slow, shuddery breath and reached for her wine. 'Just give me some details, Jace.'

Jace's mouth tightened, his eyes narrowing. 'I believe I mentioned yesterday that many of the employees here have families. The party needs to be family-friendly. Children will be invited.'

Eleanor's hand tightened around the stem of her wine glass. She didn't expect it to hurt so much to hear Jace talk of children. She realised, with a sudden laser-like dart of pain, that he could be married. Maybe he had children of his own. Maybe he just hadn't wanted *her* children.

The children she'd never have.

She had to stop thinking like this. She'd got over Jace and his betrayal—unbearable as it had been—years ago. She *had*. She'd even accepted her own loss, the heartache that she'd always carry with her. She'd moved on with her life, had made plenty of friends, developed an exciting and successful career—

'Family-friendly,' she repeated, trying to keep her mind on track. She'd forgotten that rather crucial detail in her flurry of plans. Conveniently. She preferred not to think about families—children—at all. They no longer figured in her life. At all. They couldn't.

'Yes,' Jace confirmed, and his voice held an edge now. 'As I told you yesterday. Weren't you taking notes?'

Finally goaded past her emotional endurance, Eleanor set her wine glass down with an undignified clatter. 'Perhaps I just had trouble believing a man like you could be interested in anything family-friendly,' she snapped. 'The image doesn't really fit.'

'Image?' Jace repeated silkily. 'What are you talking about, Eleanor?'

'You, Jace.' The remembered pain and hurt was boiling up, seeping through the barely healed-over scars. She stood up from the table, surprised by this sudden, intense rush of feeling. Suddenly she didn't want to keep her composure any more. She wanted it to slip, wanted Jace to see the turbulent river of emotions underneath. Even to know how much he'd hurt her. Perhaps she'd regret the impulse later, but now it was too overwhelming a need to ignore. 'You're not "family-friendly".' She held up her hands to make inverted commas, her fingers curling into claws. 'You certainly weren't when I knew you.'

Jace stood up too, his hip bumping the table, sloshing wine onto the pristine white tablecloth. With a jolt Eleanor realised he was just as angry—and emotional—as she was. Maybe even more so.

'*I* wasn't family-friendly?' he repeated in a low voice that was nearly a growl. 'And just how and when did you draw that ridiculous conclusion?'

Eleanor nearly choked in her fury and disbelief. 'Maybe when you left your apartment, left the damn *country* when I told you I was pregnant!' There was a buzzing in her ears and distantly she realised she was shouting. Loudly.

Jace let out an ugly snarl of a laugh. 'Oh, I see. How interesting, Ellie.' On his lips her name was a sneer. 'So I'm some monster that doesn't like children simply because I didn't want to take on another man's bastard.'

Eleanor's mouth dropped open. The buzzing in her ears intensified so she couldn't hear anything. Surely she must have misheard him. 'What did you say?' she asked numbly, still slack-jawed.

Jace's lip curled in contempt. 'You heard me. I knew that baby wasn't mine.'

CHAPTER THREE

THE room was silent save for the draw and tear of their own ragged breathing. Numbly Eleanor turned away from Jace, from the table with its jostled dishes and spilled wine, and walked on wooden legs to the window.

Outside the sky was the ominous grey-white that promised a storm, the world below a winter palette of browns and greys.

Another man's bastard. Jace's words echoed in his ears, over and over, so Eleanor could not frame another thought or even a word. *Another man's bastard. Bastard. Bastard. Bastard.*

She closed her eyes.

'So you have nothing to say,' Jace said coldly, and that too was an indictment.

Eleanor shook her head. Her heart was thudding sickly and her knees nearly buckled. She'd never had such a physical reaction to a single piece of information, except when—

Tell me what's wrong.

No. She wasn't going to open up that Pandora's box of memories. Not with Jace in the room, with his ugly words still reverberating through the air.

And she wasn't going to defend herself either. There was so clearly no point.

Slowly she turned around. 'No,' she said quietly. 'I have nothing to say.'

Jace nodded in grim acceptance, and Eleanor knew she'd

just confirmed the worst he'd ever thought about her. Judged again. She hadn't even realised, ever known, that she'd been judged in the first place. All these years she'd had no idea Jace had been thinking that. Believing the worst. And why? What reason had she ever given him?

She walked back to the table and reached for the attaché case she'd propped against her chair.

'I'm going to go now,' she said steadily. She was grateful her voice didn't tremble or break. 'I'll make sure Lily assigns someone else to your party.'

'What are you talking about?' Jace demanded, and Eleanor almost laughed. Did he actually think she'd work with him now? Considering what had just happened—what he thought—

She shook her head again. 'Clearly, Jace, we can't move on from the past, and it's affecting our—our work relationship.' What a ridiculous idea, as though they could have any relationship at all. 'There's no point continuing this way. Someone else will serve you better.'

'So you expect me just to forgive and forget,' Jace surmised, his voice sharp with sarcasm.

Now Eleanor did laugh, a short, humourless bark. 'No. I'm the one who can't. Forgive *or* forget.' She hoisted her bag on her shoulder and gave him a grim little smile. 'Goodbye, Jace.'

And somehow, *somehow* she managed to walk from the room with steady legs, her head held high.

Jace watched Eleanor walk away from him in stunned disbelief. He heard the click of the door shutting, the surprised murmur of his PA, the whoosh of the lift doors. And he still didn't move.

I'm the one who can't forgive or forget.

What the hell had she been talking about?

Muttering an angry oath, Jace whirled towards the window. What could Eleanor Langley possibly have to forgive? All right, perhaps he'd been ruthless in the way he'd cut her out of his life, leaving Boston—leaving her—so abruptly and absolutely. But he'd done it because the realisation that she'd been deceiving him all along had been too terrible to bear. He'd felt quite literally gutted, empty and aching inside. And meanwhile she—*she* had been trying to foist another man's child on him. Living a lie all along. She'd never really loved him.

Yet apparently Eleanor did think she had something to forget. To forgive.

What?

Impatiently Jace turned away from the window where a few random snowflakes had begun to drift down onto the asphalt. He felt restless, angry, uncertain. The last was what bothered him the most; he'd never felt doubt before. How could he? He'd known since he was fifteen years old that he was infertile.

Sterile. Like a gelded bull, or a eunuch. As good as, according to his father. For what good was a son who couldn't carry on the family name? Who had been unmanned before he'd even reached his manhood?

What use was a son like that?

Jace already knew the answer, had known the answer since his test results had come back and his father's dreams of a dynasty had crumbled to dust. Nothing. A son like that—like him—was no use at all.

He'd lived with that grim knowledge for half of his life. Felt it in every quietly despairing stare, every veiled criticism. His own infertility had consumed him before he'd even been ready to think of children, had dominated him as a boy and become part of his identity as a man. Without the ability to have children, he was useless. Worthless.

And yet now, with Ellie's words, doubt, both treacherous and strangely hopeful, crept into his mind and wound its tendrils of dangerous possibility around his thoughts. His heart.

What did Ellie have to forget? To forgive? What had she been talking about?

Half of him wanted to ignore what she had said, just move on. He'd get a different event planner, forget Eleanor Langley even existed. Never question what she said.

Never wonder.

Yet even as these thoughts raced through his brain, Jace knew he couldn't do that. Didn't even want to. Yes, it was saner, safer, but it was also aggravating as hell. He didn't want to doubt. Couldn't let himself wonder.

He needed to know.

Eleanor walked all the way back to Premier Planning's office near Madison Square Garden, oblivious to the cold wind buffeting her face and numbing her cheeks. She was oblivious to everything, every annoyed pedestrian, cellphone clamped to an ear, who was forced to move around her as she sleep-walked the twenty-three blocks to her office. She felt numb, too numb to think, to consider just what Jace had said. What he'd thought all these years.

She stood in front of the building, still numb, still reeling, and realised distantly that she couldn't return to work. Lily would be waiting, anxious for a report—or worse. Perhaps Jace had already rung. Perhaps her job was already in jeopardy.

Either way, she couldn't face it. She turned her back on ten years of professionalism and went home.

Back in the apartment she dropped her bag on the floor, kicked off her heels, and slumped into a chair, staring out into space. She didn't know how long she stayed like that for, without moving, without thinking, but the sky darkened to violet and then indigo, and her stomach rumbled. She hadn't eaten since breakfast, and that had been no more than half a bagel as she hurried to work. Yet she still couldn't summon the energy to eat. To feel. Anything. She hadn't felt this numb—the pain too consuming to allow herself to feel it—for a long time. For ten years.

Finally she stirred and went to the bathroom. She turned both taps on full and stripped off her clothes, leaving her savvy suit crumpled on the floor. Who knew if she'd need it any more?

Twenty minutes into a good soak she felt her mind start to thaw. So did her heart. So Jace assumed she'd been unfaithful, had been labouring under that unbelievable misapprehension for ten long years. No wonder he was so angry. Yet how could he be so *wrong*?

How could he have thought that of her, considering what they'd been to one another? Even the logistics of infidelity were virtually impossible; she'd spent nearly every waking moment working, at school, or with him.

Yet he'd believed it, and believed it so strongly that he'd judged her without trial, without even a conversation. He'd been so sure of her infidelity that he'd left her, left his entire life in the States, without even asking so much as a single question.

Somehow it was so much worse than what she'd thought all these years: that he'd developed a case of cold feet. In her more compassionate moments, she could understand how a twenty-two-year-old man—*boy*—with his whole life in front of him might get a little panicked at the thought of fathering a child. She understood that; what she didn't understand, had never understood, was the way he'd gone about it. Leaving so abruptly. Abandoning her without a word or even a way for him to contact him. Cellphone disconnected. No forwarding address.

It hadn't been merely a slap to the face, it had been a stab wound to the heart.

And he'd done it not because of his own inadequacy, but because of hers. Infidelity. He actually assumed she'd cheated on him.

The bath water was getting cold, and Eleanor rose from the tub. There was no point letting herself dwell on the recriminations, the regrets. If Jace Zervas had been able to believe something so atrocious and impossible about her so easily, obviously they'd never had much of a relationship at all.

And *that* was a truth she'd lived with for ten years.

She'd just slipped on her comfort pyjamas—soft, nubby fleece—when her doorbell rang. Eleanor stilled. She lived on the thirtieth floor in a building with two security personnel at the front door at all times, so no one made it to her door without her being alerted. The only option, she supposed, was a neighbour, although she'd never really got to know her neighbours. It wasn't that kind of building, and she didn't have that kind of life.

Cautiously Eleanor went to the door. She peered through the eyehole and felt her heart stop for a second before beginning a new, frenetic beating. Jace stood there.

'Eleanor?'

He sounded impatient, and it was no wonder. Eleanor realised she was hesitating for far too long. Resolutely she drew a breath and opened the door.

'What are you doing here, Jace?'

'I need to talk to you.'

She folded her arms and didn't move. She didn't feel angry now so much as resigned. 'I told you in your office I had nothing to say.'

'You may not, but I do.' He arched an eyebrow. 'Are you going to let me in?'

'How did you get my address?'

'Your boss gave it to me.'

Eleanor gave an exasperated sigh. *Of course.* Lily would do just about anything for a client, especially a rich one like Jace. 'How did you get past security?'

'I sweet-talked him.'

Eleanor snorted. 'You?'

'Andreas is manning the door tonight. He has six grandchildren back in Greece.' Jace smiled thinly. 'He showed me pictures.'

Eleanor slowly shook her head. She'd been on the end of Jace's charm once; she knew how forceful it was. And how false.

Sighing in defeat, she turned away from the door. 'Fine. Come in.'

He entered, shutting the door carefully behind him. Eleanor moved to the window, her arms creeping around her body despite her effort to maintain a cool, composed air. She felt vulnerable, exposed somehow, as if from the stark modernity of her apartment Jace could somehow guess at the emotional barrenness of her life.

Stop. She couldn't think like that. She had a job, friends, a life—

She just didn't have what mattered.

Love.

Stop.

'What do you want?'

Jace stood in the centre of her living room, seeming too big, too *much* for the space. He glanced around, and Eleanor saw him take in all the telltale signs of a single life. No jumble of shoes or coats, no piles of magazines or books. Just a single pair of heels discarded by the door. In the galley kitchen she saw her lone coffee cup from this morning rinsed and set by the sink. 'You live here alone?'

She lifted one shoulder in a shrug that couldn't help but seem defensive. 'Yes.'

He shook his head slowly. 'What about—the baby?' He spoke awkwardly, the words sounding stilted. They felt stilted to Eleanor. She didn't want him to ask. She didn't want him to know.

She didn't want to tell.

'What about the baby?' she asked evenly.

'He—or she, rather—doesn't live with you?'

'No.'

'The father retained custody?'

She gave a short, abrupt laugh. The weariness was fading away and the anger was coming back. Along with the hurt. She was tired of feeling so much, so suddenly, after ten years of being comfortably numb. She dropped her arms to her sides. 'What do you really want to talk about, Jace?'

'You said you were the one who couldn't forgive or forget. And I want to know why.' He spoke flatly, yet she saw something in his eyes she hadn't seen in ten years, something that hadn't been there yesterday or this morning. Need.

Hunger.

Why did he want to know? Why did he care?

'Because you may have felt you had just cause, but the fact that you abandoned me the very day I told you I was pregnant was a hard thing to get over.' She smiled thinly. 'Surprisingly, it seems.'

Jace shook his head, the movement one of instinctive denial. 'Ellie, you know that baby isn't—wasn't—mine.'

Anger, white-hot, lanced through her. '*I* know?' she repeated, her voice rising in incredulity. '*I* know? I'll tell you what I know, Jace, and that is that the only bastard I've ever met is you. First-class, A-plus, for thinking that.'

He took a step towards her in an action both menacing and urgent, his features twisted with what looked like pain. 'Are you telling me,' he demanded in a low voice, 'that the baby was mine? Is that what you're actually saying, Ellie?'

She lifted her chin. 'That's exactly what I'm saying, Jace. And the very fact that you could think for a moment—'

'Don't.' He held up one hand, and Eleanor saw to her shock that it trembled. 'Don't,' he repeated rawly, 'lie to me. Not now. Not again. Not about this.'

For a second Eleanor's anger gave way to another powerful emotion: curiosity. Jace faced her, his expression open and hungry. She'd never see him look so…desperate. There was more going on here than she understood.

'I'm not lying,' she said quietly. 'What makes you think I ever was?'

Jace didn't speak for a moment. His gaze held hers, searching for a truth he seemed hell-bent on disbelieving. 'Because,' he finally said, his voice little more than a ragged whisper, 'I can't have children. I've known it since I was fifteen years old.' He let out a long, slow breath before stating flatly, 'I'm infertile. Sterile.'

Eleanor stared. *I can't have children.* Such a stark and sorrowful phrase; she knew just how much. And yet coming from *Jace*…the words didn't make sense. They couldn't. Then in a sudden flash of remembrance she recalled the moment she'd told Jace she was pregnant, and how he'd stared at her so blankly, his jaw slackening, his eyes turning flat and then hard. She'd thought he'd been surprised; she'd had no idea just how stunned he must have been. Infertile. *Impossible*. It had to be. 'You must be mistaken.'

'I assure you I'm not.'

Eleanor shook her head, speechless, disbelieving. 'Well, neither am I,' she finally said. 'Mistaken, that is. I was a virgin when we got together, Jace, and I didn't sleep with another man for—a long while.' She swallowed. Years, in fact, but she wasn't about to tell him that. 'You were the only candidate.'

Jace smiled, the curving of his mouth utterly without humour. 'The facts don't add up, Ellie. Someone's lying.'

'I've told you not to call me that.' She turned away from him and stared blindly out at the Hudson River, its murky black surface just visible under the city lights. 'Why does someone have to be lying, Jace? What if you're mistaken?' She turned around. 'Did you ever—even once—think of that?'

'I'm not!' The words came out in a roar, and she stilled, surprised by the savagery.

'How can you be—?'

'Trust me,' he cut her off, the two words flat and brutal. 'I am. And if I can't have children, there must be another—' he paused, his mouth curving in an unpleasant smile '—candidate.'

Eleanor cocked her head, curiosity and anger warring within her. 'Is it easier for you to believe that?'

'What the hell do you mean?'

She shrugged, a little unnerved by Jace's anger but still refusing to be cowed. 'You prefer believing I was unfaithful to you rather than the idea that you could be wrong, that it's a mistake—'

'It's not a mistake!' Jace leaned forward, lowered his voice to a savage whisper. 'It's *impossible*.'

Eleanor blinked, discomfited by his intensity. 'How did you find out you were infertile at such a young age?' she asked slowly. 'Most men don't find out until they're married and run into trouble with conceiving, don't they—'

'I had mumps. A lingering infection, and it made me sterile.'

'And you were tested—?'

'Yes.' He bit off the word, his lips pressed together in a hard line.

'But…' Eleanor shook her head, genuinely bewildered. 'Why? Why would you be tested at such a young age?'

Jace turned away from her. He drove his hands into his pockets, his shoulders hunched, the position one of defensive misery. 'My father wanted to know,' he said gruffly, his back still to her. 'I'm an only son, as was he. The male line dies out with me.'

Eleanor didn't reply. She couldn't think of a single thing to say, for suddenly everything was making horrible sense. No wonder Jace was so sure he couldn't be the father. No wonder he'd been so hurt. No wonder the whole idea of a pregnancy—a baby—that wasn't his would be an affront, an abomination.

The male line dies out with me.

For a boy from a traditional Greek family, that had to be very hard indeed.

Regret replaced anger, and it hurt far more. She swallowed past the tightness in her throat. 'Well, perhaps you should get yourself tested again. Because I assure you, Jace, the baby was yours. Why would I lie now? What point would there be?'

Jace was silent for a long, tense moment. 'I don't know,' he finally said. 'God help me, I don't know.' Eleanor stared at him, his back to her, his head bowed, and she wondered what he must be feeling now. Could he accept he wasn't infertile, that he'd been living with an incorrect diagnosis for his entire adult life?

Would he?

It would be hope and tragedy mixed together, for what was lost, for what now could be—

But not for her. Eleanor swallowed past the tightness in her throat, closing her eyes as if that could blot out the pain. The memory. Never for her.

Jace drew in a ragged, desperate breath, his head still bowed, his back to Eleanor. He felt the rage course through him, consume him, and he didn't trust himself to speak.

The baby was his. *Could* be his. Except in his gut—perhaps even in his heart—Jace knew the truth. He saw it in Eleanor's eyes, dark with remembered pain. The baby was his.

He wasn't infertile.

And all he could feel was anger. All he could think of was the waste. His life, his family, his father. Everything had pointed to his failure as a son, as a man. He'd lived with it, let it cripple him, let it guide and restrain his choices, and for what?

For a lie? A *mistake*?

The realisation made him want to shout to the remorseless heavens, to hit something, to hurt something. Someone. *It wasn't fair.* The cry of a child, and yet it bellowed up inside him, the need so great he clamped his lips together and drew another shuddering breath.

Eleanor, he knew, would never understand. How could he explain how utterly sure he'd been of his own infertility, so that he'd been able to walk away without once considering that she'd been telling the truth? He'd always been so certain that even now he wondered. Doubted.

It can't be.

And yet if it was…

Too many repercussions, too many unspoken—unthought—hopes and fears crowded his mind, his heart. He pushed them down, unable to deal with them now, to consider what they meant, what changes to both the present and future—and, God help him, the past—they would require.

The baby was his.

The baby was his.

He had a child.

Jace whirled around again, the movement so sudden and savage that Eleanor gasped aloud and took a step towards the window.

He crossed the room in three long strides and grabbed her by the shoulders, his face thrust near hers. 'Where is the baby? If it *is* my child—'

Eleanor closed her eyes. She didn't want this. She didn't want Jace here, stirring up memories, regrets, *pain*, and for what? Yet she knew he had a right to know. She swallowed again. Her throat was so very tight. 'Was,' she whispered. 'It was.'

'What—what are you talking—?'

'It *was* your child,' she explained very quietly, and the fierce light that had ignited in Jace's eyes winked out, leaving them the colour of cold ash.

'You mean…' his hands tightened on her shoulders '…you had an abortion.'

'No!' She jerked out of his grasp, glaring at him. 'Why don't you just leap to yet another offensive assumption, Jace? You're good at that.'

He folded his arms, his expression still hard. 'What are you saying, then?'

'I had a…a miscarriage.' A bland, official-sounding word for such a heart-rending, life-changing event. She turned away from him so he wouldn't see the naked pain on her face. She felt the thickness of tears in her throat. 'I lost the baby.' She swallowed. *My little girl,* she thought, *my precious little girl.*

Jace was silent for a long moment. Eleanor stared blindly out of the window, trying not to remember. The screen, the silence, the emptiness within. 'I'm sorry,' he finally said, and she just shrugged. The silence ticked on, heavy, oppressive. 'I'm sorry,' Jace said again, the word raw, and Eleanor felt again the thickening of tears in her throat. She swallowed it down, reluctant to let Jace enter her sorrow. She didn't want to rake it up again; she didn't even want him sharing it. She was still angry. Still hurt.

'I'll still have to be tested,' he continued, 'to make sure—'

'That the baby was yours?' Eleanor filled in. 'You still don't believe me?' She shook her head in disbelief. 'Just when would I have had this other affair, Jace? I spent every waking—and sleeping—moment with you for six *months*.'

'You don't understand—' Jace began in a low voice, but Eleanor didn't want to hear.

'No, I don't. I don't understand how you could think for a moment that I was unfaithful to you. But even if you did, because I suppose you must have had some kind of *trust* issue, I don't understand how you could walk away without a word.' Her voice shook; so did her body. 'Without a single *word*.'

'Eleanor—'

'It doesn't matter. I don't want to hear your explanations now. They don't matter.' She took a deep, shuddering breath and forced herself to sound calm. To feel it. 'It's ten years ago, Jace. Ten years. It really is time we both moved on.'

He was silent, and when she looked at him she saw how drawn and tired and *sad* he looked. Well, too bad. She hardened her heart, because she didn't want to feel sorry for him. She didn't want to feel anything; it hurt too much. 'If only I'd known,' he murmured, and she shook her head.

'Don't.' She didn't want him to open up the painful possibilities of what if, if only… No, they were too dangerous. Too hard even to think about now. 'And it doesn't even matter anyway,' she continued, her voice sharp. 'You didn't trust me enough to tell me any of this, or give either of us a chance to explain. That's what this was really about.'

Jace's brows snapped together, his body tensing, and Eleanor knew he was poised to argue. Again. She couldn't take any more, didn't have the energy for another round. 'Go get tested or whatever it is you need to do,' she told him. 'Satisfy your own curiosity. You don't need to tell me about it.' She paused, her voice sharpening again in spite of her best efforts to sound reasonable. '*I* know who the father was.'

Jace stared at Ellie's hard face, derision in every line, her eyes dark with scorn. He felt a scalding sense of shame rush through him. This hard, polished woman, this glossy professional who lifted her chin and dared him to feel sympathy or compassion or dreaded pity, was a product of his own judgment. His own failure.

If he'd stayed with Ellie…if he'd seen her through the miscarriage…would she be a different woman? Would she have stayed the same?

It was a pointless question. As Eleanor herself had said, this was all ten years too late. They'd both moved on. They'd both changed. He certainly wasn't the same foolish boy who'd let himself be besotted, who had eagerly fallen in love because the experience had been so intoxicating, so vital, so different from what he'd known.

Who had a heart to be broken.

No, he wasn't that same man. He'd changed, hardened, and so had Ellie. *Eleanor.* They were different people now, and the only thing they had in common was loss.

The loss of their baby. A sudden, new grief threatened to swamp him, and to his shock he felt the sting of tears in his eyes, the ache in the back of his throat. He forced the feeling down, refusing to give into such an emotion. He never cried. In the fifteen or so years since his life had changed for ever—or at least until now—he'd developed a foolproof way of dealing with his father's disappointment. He never acted as if he cared. Whether it was a flat, emotionless response, or a carefree, laughing one, either way he kept his heart off-limits. He remained detached. He *had*, until Eleanor.

Somehow Eleanor had slipped through the defences he'd erected—that charming, laughing exterior—and found the man underneath. He wondered if she even knew how much she'd affected him.

And how had he affected her? In a sudden, painful burst of insight he pictured her in his apartment building, twenty years old and pregnant, realising he'd gone. He'd abandoned her utterly, and she'd been innocent.

Innocent.

He'd never, for a moment or even a second, considered that the child—their child—might have been his. This infertility was so much a part of him, a weight that had been shackled to him for so long, he'd never considered existing without it. He'd never even hoped for such a possibility.

And yet now for it to be given to him, and taken away, virtually in the same breath was too much to consider. To accept. He was left speechless, his mind spinning in dizzying circles, his heart thudding as if he'd just finished a sprint.

He didn't know what to think. To feel. And he was afraid—yes, afraid—to open up the floodgates of his own heart and mind to all the possibilities, all the realisations, all the regret and guilt and hope and fear. They would consume him; he would have nothing left. Nothing he could count on or control. He couldn't do that. Not yet, maybe not ever.

He needed to get this situation back under control, Jace knew, and there was only one way to do that.

'So,' Jace said, and was glad to hear how even his voice sounded. 'Let's talk about this party.'

CHAPTER FOUR

'WHAT?' Eleanor heard the screech of her own voice and briefly closed her eyes. She opened them and shook her head. 'No.'

Jace arched an eyebrow in challenge. 'Why not? You didn't seem to have a problem with planning the party before.'

'You can't be serious. After everything—'

'We're professionals, Eleanor.' Jace's voice was hard, and Eleanor saw a bleak darkness in his eyes. She felt its answer in herself, and she wondered if Jace was trying to prove something to himself, just as she was. *The past is finished. It doesn't matter. I'm not hurt.*

But she was. And she was so tired of pretending she wasn't. Yet even so she couldn't admit that to Jace. She felt exposed enough, considering all she'd already revealed. She wasn't about to say anything more. 'Of course we're professionals, Jace. But I simply think it would be sensible—not to mention more productive—to have a colleague plan your event.'

'I don't.'

Why was he doing this? She shook her head again. 'I told you at your office—'

'That you were quitting? Lucky for you I didn't communicate that to your boss. I don't think she would have been pleased. And somehow I had a feeling you might change your mind.' His mouth twisted sardonically, his eyes glinting.

Eleanor didn't answer. She knew just how displeased Lily would have been. She might have thrown her entire career away in a single, emotional moment, and Jace at least had had the presence of mind not to let her do it.

She supposed she should be grateful.

Eleanor walked slowly back to the window. It had become her place of retreat; either that or she was simply backed into a corner. 'I don't understand why you want to do this,' she said quietly. 'Or what can be gained—for either of us.'

Jace shrugged one powerful shoulder. 'You're the best planner. Or so I was told.'

'You didn't even like my ideas,' Eleanor protested numbly. What she really wanted to say was, *Why doesn't being with me hurt you?* She felt his presence like an agony, exquisitely painful. And he wanted her to plan his *party*?

'I just know you can do better.'

She shook her head, even as she acknowledged that he was right. She *could* do better. She'd fought long and hard to get to where she was in her business and stay there. And she wasn't about to throw it all away simply because Jace had come back into her life—however briefly—and stirred up some old memories. She could shove them down again. She could handle this party. She could handle Jace. Doing it would help her feel more in control, and God knew she needed to feel that again.

She felt as if she were spinning out of it, and she couldn't stand the sense of powerlessness. She'd felt that before, when Jace had walked out of her life. When the ultrasound technician had sorrowfully shaken her head, and the doctor had come in to give her lots of important-sounding words and clinical, medical terms.

She wasn't going to feel it now.

She turned around. Jace gazed at her, waiting, assessing. She had no idea why he still wanted her to plan his wretched party, what he hoped to gain or prove. Or was the past nothing more than a finished chapter of a sad story? Could he actually move on so quickly, *minutes* after she'd told him the truth? She made herself not care. She'd done that before, plenty of times, starting when she was a little girl and her mother had worked late again and again, missing plays and soccer matches and anything important. When Jace had walked away, when she'd lost her little girl, when life had seemed empty and endless and without hope—she'd survived by making herself not care. By blanking her mind to any thought—any possibility—that was too painful. Too hard. And she could keep doing it. Keep surviving. Keep not caring.

Eleanor smiled coolly. 'Fine, Jace. I'll plan your party. Satisfied?'

'Getting there.'

'And it's late. I'd like to go to bed.' Too late she realised how laced those words were with innuendo—and remembrance. And so did Jace. She saw it in the subtle flaring of his eyes, the way they turned to sleepy silver. And before she could stop herself, her mind flashed images from a lifetime ago—a lifetime with Jace. Lying in his arms, tracing circles on the bare, bronze skin of his chest. Laughing, stretching like a cat, sleepy and secure. Sated. Loving every moment of being with him, because she'd been young and naive enough to think it was real and that it would never end.

Eleanor swallowed. 'I'm tired,' she said as an explanation, but it came out in a whisper. Jace smiled.

'So am I.'

Was she imagining the current that suddenly seemed to run between them, alive and electric? She must be, because surely, *surely* there was nothing between them. After everything that had happened—after everything she had endured—there could be nothing between them now.

Yet that didn't stop her from remembering just how good it had once been.

'Goodnight, Jace,' Eleanor said, and her voice, to her relief, sounded flat and final and almost cold. Jace ignored her.

He took a step towards her. Eleanor held her breath. She didn't speak, didn't move. Didn't protest. Another step, and he was only inches away. He lifted his hand and she braced herself for his touch, welcomed it even, wondering what it would feel like after all these years. What he would feel like.

And even as she stood there, still and silent, *waiting* for him to touch her, he dropped his hand, smiling almost sadly. 'Goodnight, Ellie,' he said, and this time Eleanor didn't try to correct him.

She watched him leave, not realising until the door had shut that she was still holding her breath. She let it out in a long, shuddery rush.

She could do this. She had to.

Jace strode from Eleanor's apartment, his body filled with a restless energy, his mind teeming with both possibility and fury. He was angry at himself, at fate, at life itself.

So much waste. So much wrong.

Guilt rushed into the corners of his mind, the empty spaces in his heart. He could hardly bear to think what Eleanor must have felt, what she'd endured alone.

If only—

Two desperate and dangerous words.

If only he'd known. If only he'd waited and said something, asked her—

If only. If only.

There was no such thing as *if only*. There was only regret.

And hope.

Jace shook his head in silent disbelief. Hope had long since become an unfamiliar concept. What on earth could he hope for? Love, family, children—he'd turned his back on them all. Was he now actually thinking that he could change that? Change himself? It would not be so easy.

For years work had been his only respite, his only comfort. He'd come to New York as a favour to Leandro Atrikides, and as a favour to his father. He'd clean up the family mess and then he'd go home to Greece.

And forget about Eleanor Langley…just as he had once before.

Except he'd never forgotten her, not really. She'd always lurked on the fringes of his consciousness, memories drifting and dancing through his mind even when he tried to push them away. She lingered there now.

He recalled her scent, something young and girlish and flowery. He didn't think she used the same perfume now. And her hair had been wild and curly and artless, not her current glossy bob. He remembered the feel of those curls bouncing against his chest as she laughed in his arms.

Now Eleanor Langley looked totally different from the young woman he'd fallen in love with. He wondered if the changes were intentional. Had she transformed herself into this hardened career woman on purpose? Or had it happened gradually, without her even realising, the product of ten years' ceaseless striving in this heartless city?

And what about underneath?

Had her heart changed?

Ten years ago he'd judged her heart. He'd thought her cold and scheming and had walked away without ever finding out the truth. He'd thought he'd known it. He'd been so sure…

Now every certainty had been scattered, leaving him both hopeful and afraid. He didn't know what the future could hold, for him or Eleanor. He didn't even dare think, or question or wonder.

If only…

Jace left Eleanor's building, clamping his mind down on that thought as he walked down the dark, empty street.

Eleanor woke slowly, swimming upwards through consciousness from a deep and dreamless sleep. She blinked slowly; her room seemed to be obscured by a soft white haze.

As she sat up in bed, pushing her tangled mass of hair out of her eyes, she realised why. It was snowing. She scrambled out of bed and hurried to the window, pressing her hand against the cold glass. Outside the city's skyscrapers were lost in a snowstorm. Huge white flakes drifted down and the streets were already covered, the parked cars no more than white humps.

Snow. She smiled, suddenly feeling as excited and hopeful as a child when she'd had a rare snow day. There had been a blizzard once, when she was nine, and her mother had been forced to stay home from work. Eleanor still remembered that magical moment when her mother had decided to stay home for the day. The telephones hadn't been working, and, according to the television, no one was going anywhere. For a moment that pinched look had left her mother's face and she'd smiled and shrugged. 'I guess we'll have a snow day,' she'd said.

They'd trudged to Central Park through several feet of fluffy whiteness armed with a metal baking sheet—all the sledges had been sold out at the shop—and gone sledging on Cedar Hill near Seventy-Ninth Street. The feeling of flying down the hill, the world no more than a blur of muted colour, her mother's arms wrapped around her, was one Eleanor had never forgotten. She carried it with her like a treasure.

Snow. This sudden snowstorm felt like a treasure, a promise, a gift. Snow covered up all the grime and grit and hard concrete of the city, all the memories and regrets. It was a new beginning. A new hope. She didn't have to think about what had happened before, didn't have to carry the heavy, unbearable weight of ten years of memories or last night's conversation with Jace. She'd let the snow fall over it, cloaking it in whiteness, hiding it from herself.

Suddenly, certainly, Eleanor knew how to make this party just what Jace wanted. What she wanted. Smiling with a new determination, she turned away from the window.

She soon became immersed in organisation, making calls, checking facts and details, and arranging the most amazing party Jace Zervas could ever imagine. The party of her career.

She loved the buzz of creating something, seeing it emerge from her own imagination, and this party in particular was both a challenge and a dream. She had just days to conjure something spectacular.

The amount of work also kept her from thinking. Remembering. She was grateful for the activity that kept her from dwelling on the pain Jace had raked up, the regrets that still lingered on the fringes of her mind.

If only I'd known...

In her mind she never let Jace finish that sentence.

Every night she fell into bed, too exhausted to think or wonder, yet even so in that vulnerable moment before sleep overtook her she found herself picturing Jace's face, both as it had been ten years ago, young and smiling, and as it was now, determined and harsh. She remembered that shiver of electric awareness when he'd been in her apartment, when she had thought—perhaps even hoped—that he might touch her, and the memory carried her into the cocoon of sleep and insinuated itself into her dreams.

The day before the party Eleanor spent the afternoon making sure everything was in place at the event site. So much of planning an event like this was simply getting on the phone, putting in orders, cajoling and commanding at turns. Now the real fun began: making the magic.

'It's so unusual to have a party here at this time of year,' Laura, the woman who managed the boathouse in Central Park, remarked as Eleanor went over the party details with her. 'Especially with a request for the outside terrace. We're completely booked for spring and summer, but December...'

'I know,' Eleanor agreed. It was part of the reason she'd just chosen the park's boathouse as the venue; most other places had already been booked. And it was perfect for the kind of party she had planned. She surveyed the room, taking a mental count of the chairs and tables. 'My client is looking for unusual,' she explained, satisfied with the arrangements so far.

'It won't be too cold?' Laura asked dubiously. Although

the boathouse had inside seating, its most spectacular feature was the pillared terrace overlooking the park's lake. Now the lake was frozen solid, and in the distance Eleanor could see the Angel of Bethesda fountain still shrouded in snow.

'I hope not,' she said cheerfully. 'Of course, we're working on that.' She'd ordered electric heaters to be placed on the terrace in strategic spots, to warm up cold little hands and feet.

'Well, all right,' Laura said, still sounding doubtful, and Eleanor pushed away the thought that perhaps she was in fact crazy. Ever since she'd first seen those few fat flakes drifting down, she'd been gripped by a vision, a *memory*, and she'd let it drive her through one of the most intense working weeks she'd ever experienced.

It left little time or room for doubt. Yet now as Laura went back to her office and Eleanor was left alone in the boathouse's Lake Room, she wondered if Jace would think this party was impressive enough. *Suitable.*

And she wondered why she should even care.

Sighing, Eleanor shook her head and walked over to the glass doors that led out onto the terrace. It was too late for doubts or regrets; the party was tomorrow night. Everything had been ordered, prepared, paid for. The invitations, in the shape of snowflakes, had been sent out to all the employees. All that was left was the doing.

Eleanor turned the door handle and pushed it open; a gust of freezing air hit her in the face. Drawing in a deep lungful of the cold, frosty air, she stepped out onto the terrace.

The sky was just darkening to violet, the sun disappearing behind the stark, bare branches that fringed the park. Eleanor stood by the railing, surveying the silent, frozen lake, the park empty of tourists or pedestrians on this cold evening. It never ceased to amaze her that she stood in nearly the exact centre of a city of eight million people, and the only sound was the creak and crack of shifting ice.

It's going to be okay.

She let herself relax, unloosen all the tensed, tightly held parts of herself. She didn't let herself relax too often; she knew from experience it was too hard once you let go to get it all back together again. Yet now, just for a moment, she let herself be still, serene—or as close to it as she could be.

It's going to be okay.

She wasn't even sure what was going to be okay: the party? The future? Something more nebulous that she couldn't yet name? Eleanor had no answers.

'They told me I'd find you here.'

Eleanor tensed, all the loosely held parts of herself coming together in a cold, hard ball. She turned slowly around to survey Jace.

He stood in the doorway, dressed in a navy suit and wool overcoat, a briefcase in one hand. His cheeks were reddened with cold, emphasising the silvery glint of his eyes and the inky blackness of his hair.

'On the terrace?' Eleanor said a bit stupidly, for despite her cool smile her mind seemed to have slowed down, only able to process how amazing he looked.

Jace smiled crookedly. It reminded her of the way he used to smile, back when they were students. Lovers. He hadn't smiled like that in the last week; all his smiles had been cold or calculated, a cruel curving of the lips. This one was real, lopsided, and yet somehow sad. The memories still lay between them, heavy and unspoken. Eleanor wondered if they would always be there. 'Actually, in the restaurant. But the door was open, so I figured you came out for a breath of fresh air.'

'Very fresh,' Eleanor agreed, and Jace smiled again. Her heart turned right over, a flip-flop that was both exciting and a little alarming. She didn't want to respond to him, not physically, not emotionally. She didn't want to feel anything at all. Yet somehow, even now, after everything they'd been through, after everything she'd endured, she still did.

He set his briefcase down by the door and joined her at the railing. 'How's it going?'

'Good.' She gave a quick little laugh; it sounded sharp.

She knew what that laugh was: a defence mechanism. She inched away from him. 'You haven't been checking up on me all week. I expected an email or phone call to make sure the arrangements were *acceptable*.' Her emphasis on the word, Eleanor knew, sounded petty.

'I thought it best,' Jace said after a second's hesitation, and Eleanor saw his fingers tighten on the railing.

And before she could stop herself, Eleanor whispered, 'Why didn't you just get someone else, Jace?' Her voice sounded little and lost.

'I don't know.' He stared out at the frozen lake, his features harshening once more. 'I didn't want to walk away from you…like that.'

Like before. Her heart turned over again. It was, she thought ruefully, as desperate and flailing as a dying fish. She averted her face as she replied, 'It would have been easier.'

Jace turned away from the railing and the lake, and Eleanor knew that the conversation—*that* conversation—was over. 'It looks like you've done a fabulous job, at any rate,' he said, his voice brisk and light. Eleanor felt equal and infuriating amounts of disappointment and relief. She really didn't want to talk about the past, about *them*, yet here she was, ripping off scabs, opening wounds.

'It's cold out here.' The lake, she saw, was now cloaked in darkness. Above the trees lights winked on in the elegant apartment buildings lining Fifth Avenue. 'I should go back inside, check on the details before I return tomorrow.'

'All right,' Jace agreed, and he followed her back into the Lake Room. Eleanor didn't look at him as she consulted her list, mindlessly scanning the endless items she'd assembled for the party. She felt rather than saw Jace, still standing by the door, watching her. Even though he stood halfway across the room, she imagined she could feel the heat emanating from his body, winding around her own heart and warming her from the inside.

'There's still a lot to do,' she told him, her eyes fixed

firmly on her list. She felt a strange new tension crackling between them, snapping inside her. A sexual tension, and she wasn't prepared for it. She'd spent ten years being angry at Jace Zervas; she wasn't ready to feel anything else. She didn't want to. 'I'll have to be back here early in the morning,' she told him brightly, at least half aware that she was starting to babble. 'Setting up. There's a lot of outside work—'

'Outside?' Jace asked, taking a step closer. 'What's outside?'

'Snow,' Eleanor said simply, and looked up.

Mistake. Jace was looking at her so intently, yet it was an intensity she felt rather than saw, as if his gaze reached right down into her soul and touched it. Held it, even. In that moment she remembered—she *felt*—the power he'd held over her ten years ago, when she'd given him everything. Her body, her dreams, her very life. Her happiness. And for a little while he'd kept them, treasured them, or seemed to. For such a short, sweet time life had seemed so wonderful.

Somehow she found a way to drag her gaze from his. She didn't want to feel that way again. It *was* wonderful, it was captivating, and it was also extremely dangerous. If you gave someone your happiness, you might never see or feel it again.

'Snow?' Jace repeated, the word a question. 'What does this party have to do with snow?'

'Everything.' Eleanor looked back at her list, although the words blurred in front of her. She was tired, exhausted, and she probably couldn't do much good here. Yet the thought of going home made her feel a little sad. A little lonely. She could call Allie, go out for a drink—

'Eleanor?' Jace broke into her thoughts. 'You look a million miles away.'

She looked up, distracted, discomfited, because she knew why she didn't want to go home, or out, or anywhere but where Jace Zervas was.

He still held this awful, awful power over her; she was still captive. The thought was utterly aggravating.

'Sorry.' She forced herself to give him her sunny, and rather impersonal, smile, falling back on professional ploys she knew well. 'Snow, yes. When it blizzarded the other day, I thought how much fun snow is for children, especially city children, who don't see all that much of it. Winter for us— them—usually just means cold and a lot of grey slush.'

'And?'

'So I thought a party centred around snow—building snowmen, sledging, that sort of thing—would be fun. Family-friendly,' she reminded him, the stress on the word only slightly edged. Even now, it hurt. She summoned her professional smile. 'Some of my happiest childhood memories have to do with snow.'

'Really.' Jace took a step towards her. Even though he was still a good ten feet away, Eleanor felt he was too close. She made herself not move. 'I never knew that,' he said quietly.

'Well, snow days, you know. No school.'

'You didn't like school?'

She shrugged. 'What kid doesn't want a snow day?'

'Did you build snowmen? Go sledging?' He arched an eyebrow. 'Somehow I can't see your mother doing that.' He paused. 'Based on how you described her to me, of course.'

Did he remember, after all these years? Eleanor did. She remembered lying in Jace's arms, probably boring him with the silly little details of her life, her family. How she resented her mother for working so much, for being so hard and stern, for never giving her a father. She'd had an anonymous sperm donor instead, the easy, convenient way for a career woman to have a child. She'd even told Jace how she'd always insist on her own child knowing its father—

Ironic, that.

'Once she did—' She stopped. She wasn't ready to share that memory. 'Anyway, you don't know everything about me, Jace.'

'Once,' he repeated softly, moving towards her, 'I thought

I did.' He took another step closer to her. She saw a dark urgency in his eyes, felt its desperate answer in herself.

Why was she thinking like this? Feeling like this? Breathless and buzzy and so achingly aware?

'No, you didn't,' Eleanor informed him, keeping her voice curt. *Focus.* Focus on what Jace was saying, rather than how wonderful he looked. How close he was. How she could take one step—maybe two—and be in his arms.

Eleanor turned away, busying herself with the already fastened clasp of her attaché case. 'Admittedly, I made a fool of myself,' she continued in that same curt voice, 'telling you every empty thing that came into my head, but there was plenty you didn't know about me.'

'Like what?' Jace challenged softly. He'd moved even closer and she could feel him again, his heat and his strength, the sheer power radiating from him, making her, absurdly, want to lean on it. Lean on him. Already she could imagine his arms enfolding her, his chin resting on her head as he used to do—

Eleanor straightened. 'Like the fact that I wouldn't lie,' she said shortly.

Jace stilled, and the room crackled with a new kind of tension. A chilling remoteness that made Eleanor feel as cold as she'd been on the terrace.

'Right,' Jace said, and his voice sounded distant. 'Of course.' Eleanor forced herself to say nothing. No apologies, no excuses. No regrets. 'You've changed,' he said after a moment, and she tensed.

'I've been saying that all along.'

'You're the kind of person you never wanted to be,' Jace told her quietly. Eleanor froze, her mind shocked into numbness, and then she whirled around.

'That's a rather arrogant statement,' she said, her voice coldly furious. 'Not to mention incredibly rude.'

'You told me,' Jace replied steadily, 'that you never wanted to be like your mother.'

'You've never even *met* my mother—'

'You told me she was an event planner, the best in her field. Never missed a day of work. Never made a softball practice.'

Eleanor's breath came out in a slow, surrendered hiss. *'Stop—'*

'Consumed by her career, hardened and weary and lonely,' Jace finished. Each word was an indictment, delivered in a terrible, matter-of-fact tone. 'I could be looking right at her.'

Eleanor felt her face drain of colour. Her fingers, clutching the strap of her attaché so tightly, were aching and numb. She hated that Jace had assessed her so thoroughly, so damningly. She hated that he was right.

'You don't know anything,' she said, the words forced out of a throat that had closed in on itself, tight with tears. She hated too that he'd made her so emotional, when for ten years she'd managed to be as cool and professional and feelingless as ice. As snow.

'Don't I?' Jace took a step closer. Eleanor saw compassion on his face, softening those taut lines, turning his eyes to a soft, sympathetic grey. 'What made you change so much, Ellie?'

A single stab of fury streaked through her, startling her out of numbness. 'Even now you don't know the answer to that question?' she demanded, her voice harsh with accusation. 'I'll tell you what changed me, Jace. You did.'

His eyes widened, his jaw slackening for the briefest of seconds. 'Ellie—'

'And I told you, don't call me that. I stopped being Ellie the day I went to your apartment building and nobody was there.' She saw him give a little shake of his head, and she wanted to scream at his arrogance. He had no idea what she'd been through. No idea at all. He'd chosen to damn her and miss it all. 'So don't call me that again,' she informed him brutally, 'because that Ellie? The one you think you knew so well? She no longer exists. She hasn't for ten years.'

And with that, leaving Jace still shocked and speechless, Eleanor turned and left the room.

CHAPTER FIVE

EVERYTHING was ready. Or, Eleanor amended silently, as ready as it ever would be. She glanced around the dining room; the first guests were scheduled to arrive in just ten minutes.

She'd spent the entire day at the boathouse, arranging centrepieces and party favours, checking to make sure the sound system worked and the band, who had arrived an hour ago, had everything they needed. She'd visited the kitchen several times to check on the food, and just fifteen minutes ago she'd finally retired to the Ladies to freshen up and change into her cocktail dress. She'd bypassed her standard LBD, classic but boring, in favour of a spangled silver sheath dress that glittered when she moved. By the time the party rolled round, event planners were meant to fade into the background, not take centre stage. Yet Eleanor hadn't been able to resist this dress. It made her feel like a snowflake. And she needed to feel good, craved that little pleasure because ever since she'd seen Jace last night she'd been out of sorts, emotionally edgy and drained at turns. He'd thrown her completely off balance, and she hated it. One minute she felt coldly furious, the next aggravatingly aware. She hated the flip-flop of her moods, her own body. She hated that Jace had caused this, that he was the source of her weakness.

She straightened a few napkins, moved a few of the freshly cut pussy-willow branches that made the stark yet elegant centrepieces for the table. The colour of the soft grey buds reminded her of Jace's eyes.

Forcing her mind away from that train of thought, she glanced outside at the terrace, where snow had been carted in to make playful mounds, ready to be turned into snowmen and igloos. A special kids' cocoa bar with four different kinds of hot chocolate and several flavours of marshmallows and whipped cream had been set out by the electric heater.

Family-friendly.

She didn't normally do parties with children, and she'd been surprised how much she had enjoyed it. Surprised and a little sad, for children surely were not in her future. She'd accepted that long ago, had had years to live with it, yet now, with Jace back in her life—for however short a time—the pain was fresh again. Did you ever *truly* heal?

She heard a sound at the door, and with both relief and a little anxiety she realised the first guests were arriving. The party had started.

Jace stood at the threshold of the Lake Room, gazing in amazed wonder at the transformed space. The dining room was the epitome of understated elegance, strung with fairy lights, everything silver and white and crystalline. Like snow. He took in the long, graceful branches of pussy willows in their crystal vases, the snowflake ornaments at every child's place, and then glanced outside where children were delighting in playing with the mounds of snow, their faces already happily smeared with chocolate.

It was perfect.

He was only sorry to have missed the beginning, both for Eleanor's sake and that of Leandro Atrikides. Already he saw the speculative, sideways looks employees slid him, wary and uncertain. It had been Leandro's damn son Talos who had kept him from being prompt; the greedy bastard was still angling for a bigger payout.

Jace suppressed a sigh. Sometimes he wished he'd never involved himself in this unholy mess; Leandro's avaricious children had made a near ruin of his company. Jace's buyout had been little more than a mercy mission.

Yet if he hadn't come to New York, he wouldn't have seen Eleanor again…

And he was glad he had.

Wasn't he?

He realised he was searching for her through the crowds, had in fact been doing so since he'd arrived. He'd been thinking about her since he'd seen her last night, since she'd damned him with those words:

That Ellie? The one you think you knew so well? She no longer exists.

And it was all, utterly his fault. He was to blame for making Eleanor Langley the woman she was now.

You're the kind of person you never wanted to be.

Harsh words, and he knew he'd hurt her by saying them. But he couldn't take them back. He wouldn't. Yet what could he do about it? How could he help her?

And even if he did help her, somehow, wasn't he just doing it to make himself feel better? Still selfish.

Jace moved through the crowds, scanning the throng for a glimpse of Eleanor.

And then he saw her, and his head emptied of thoughts. She stood by the window, surveying the party scene with a preoccupied air, and yet despite the tiny frown between her brows she looked lovely. Breathtaking in a shimmery dress that moved like liquid silver, encasing a slender body Jace remembered and knew so well. His palms suddenly itched to slide along that silky material and find the curve of her hip, the dip of her waist. To pull her towards him, to have her come to him, unresisting, unrepentant.

To feel Ellie in his arms again.

'Eleanor!'

Eleanor turned, nerves fluttering low in her belly as she saw Jace coming towards her. It was a feeling that was both familiar and strange, for the nerves were not caused by anxiety, but anticipation. Even though they'd parted on such harsh terms last night, her body still leapt when she saw him. Almost as if she were *glad* to see him. Even though she shouldn't be.

He stopped in front of her, reaching out with both hands to clasp hers. Eleanor accepted his touch—his hands were warm, dry, and strong, his fingers folding over hers—without even thinking about what she was doing. Part of her brain knew she should step back, smile coolly, and remain safely distant. Yet that part of her had fallen silent and still. She did nothing.

He was smiling at her with warm admiration, his gaze sweeping her from the top of her elegant chignon to the tips of her rhinestone-encrusted stiletto sandals, and it did something rather pleasant and shivery to her insides. It also kept her from forming a single coherent thought.

'You look magnificent.'

'So do you,' Eleanor blurted, and then blushed. But he did, she couldn't deny it. He wore a dark grey silk suit, his crimson tie a festive splash of colour, the expensive material emphasising his powerful frame, a body she knew and remembered. A body she had once loved.

'And this party is wonderful,' Jace continued in that same warm voice, a voice she also remembered, low and honeyed, sliding over her senses.

'Thank you,' she murmured, and slipped her hands from his. Her brain was reminding her why this wasn't a good idea. Why she needed to remain poised, polished. Professional.

'Very unique.'

'That's what you wanted.' She realised she sounded a little sharp; she felt sharp, as if she were nothing but edges. She softened her words with a smile even as she took a step away. 'Everyone is about to sit down for dinner, so I should go see to a few things—'

Jace nodded his acceptance. 'I'm sorry I was late.'

'You can be late to your own party if you want.' Damn, she still sounded defensive. Why did Jace still affect her in so many ways? Her hands tingled from his touch. Her heart hurt. And the fact that he had been late hurt too. It shouldn't matter. She shouldn't care. She'd spent ten years making sure she didn't care.

Yet apparently she still did.

'I'd better go,' she said, and turned quickly away before Jace could say anything more.

A minor dilemma in the kitchen—a shortage of vegan meals—kept her occupied for the next while, and she managed to avoid Jace as she moved around the room, making sure everyone was happy and fed. Yet even so her gaze kept sliding to him of its own accord. He was seated at the head table, his head bent as he chatted and laughed with the guest on his right, a curvaceous brunette poured into an emerald-green cocktail dress. She was, Eleanor knew from the guest list, Leandro Atrikides's daughter, Kristina. She looked as if she wanted to gobble up Jace in one delicious bite.

And, Eleanor told herself, so what if she did? She was *not* jealous. Jealousy would be both pointless and absurd. She didn't *care* what Jace did, or with whom he did it. She couldn't. Eleanor turned away, smiled and chatted with a young couple five tables away from Jace and made sure not to look at him again.

At the end of the meal, just before Eleanor was about to cue the music for dancing, she heard the sharp, crystalline clang of a fork tapped against a wine glass and the room fell warily silent.

Jace rose from his seat.

Eleanor held her breath.

'Thank you all for coming,' Jace began in a melodious voice that flowed over her and the rest of his audience. 'It is a pleasure and an honour to be among you today.' He let his gaze rove over the room, warm and smiling. Eleanor stepped back away from the table, into the shadows. She wasn't sure why she didn't want Jace to see her—or if he even would— but she felt safer against the wall, away from the light. 'I'm very grateful for your presence,' Jace continued, 'especially in this difficult period of change.' Eleanor saw people shift in their seats, heard a few murmured whispers. Jace must have felt the sudden, palpable tension in the room, although he gave no sign of it. He smiled easily and kept talking.

'I want to assure you that I will do everything in my power to ensure a smooth transition, and that it is my first concern to uphold the integrity of this company, which Leandro Atrikides instilled nearly half a century ago.' He paused, letting his gaze linger on a few faces, then looked up to scan the entire audience. Eleanor retreated even further, so her back came up against the wall. 'But this evening is a time for celebration, and I am delighted to see all of you—' here he smiled at a sleepy child lolling against her mother's arms '—enjoying yourselves. So let me take a moment to thank the person who made it all happen, and in the space of a single week. Eleanor?' Her name was a question, and Eleanor blinked, stunned, speechless.

She'd been thanked before, although not very often. Event planners were meant to be invisible, as if the party magically put itself together. That was the goal. Yet here was Jace, extending his hand, smiling warmly, and looking right at her.

Somehow, even though she was skulking in the shadows like some shamed wallflower, he'd found her. And under the admiring heat of his gaze, Eleanor felt as if she'd stepped straight into the spotlight.

She heard people shift and murmur yet again, and knew her silence was becoming ridiculous. And so unlike her. She was professional. This was professional.

Even if it didn't feel like it.

Clearing her throat, she stepped away from the wall as a patter of applause fell around her like rain. She gave a little nod of acceptance. 'Thank you, Mr Zervas.' His name stuck in her throat.

'And thank you,' Jace replied. 'This couldn't have happened without you.'

She nodded again, jerkily this time, and stepped back into the shadows. To her relief the conversation resumed, and she was forgotten. Yet when she looked up she saw Jace was still gazing straight at her, and the look in his eyes—something both fierce and primal—made her legs so weak that she sagged helplessly against the wall once more.

She managed to avoid him for the next hour, although why she was avoiding him at all, Eleanor had no idea. What was she scared of? They'd parted so harshly last night, and while her mind reminded her of that painful conversation, her body tingled with awareness and memory. Desire, even.

Eleanor stopped in mid-stride on the way to the kitchen and blew out a long, slow breath as she acknowledged her attraction to Jace. Her aggravating and overwhelming attraction. It shouldn't even surprise her, really. Ten years ago she'd been overwhelmed by desire for him from the moment he'd entered the coffee shop where she'd been a barista and asked for a latte in that delicious Greek accent. Even after they'd been dating for several months, he'd still had the power to leave her speechless and desperate with longing in a matter of minutes. Why should that change?

As long as she reminded herself that her body's reaction to Jace was purely biological, chemical, nothing more than hormones or pheromones or whatever those things were—

'I'm almost starting to think you're hiding from me.'

Eleanor stiffened. Ahead of her the kitchen loomed, bustling, bright, safe. The hallway was narrow, dark, and empty. Except for her and Jace.

She turned around slowly, taking in his powerful frame, his immaculate suit. He smiled, that sleepy, suggestive smile she knew so well. She'd teased him that he knew it, and he always acted innocent and even affronted. Now she had no doubt: he knew. He knew the power of that smile, how it made her feel. What it had once made her do. And perhaps what it could make her do again. That was why she was avoiding him.

'Hiding from you?' she repeated, forcing a light little laugh. 'Hardly, Jace. Just busy.'

'Of course,' he murmured, still smiling, and Eleanor had

a feeling he wasn't fooled. Even if it was true; she *was* busy. Although maybe not quite that busy. 'Still,' he continued, making Eleanor tense again, 'surely you have a few moments for me? For a dance?'

'A dance?' she repeated blankly, and his smile deepened, revealing a dimple in his cheek. She'd forgotten about that dimple; he hadn't smiled widely enough in the last week for her to see it.

Yet even though he was smiling now, even though he was looking at her with that seductive sleepiness she remembered so well, she sensed something underneath. Something deeper and darker, marred by sorrow. He hadn't forgotten. The past still loomed between them. No matter how light he kept his voice, Eleanor sensed he was pretending—hiding—perhaps as much as she was.

'Yes, you know? Dance?' He held out his arms as if he were leading an imaginary dance partner and did a quick box-step in the hallway. Eleanor folded her arms, trying to be resolute and regretful and failing. She was actually smiling, although perhaps not as widely as Jace. Yet it felt good to smile, felt right to leave the cares and regrets behind, if only for a night.

'I don't really dance.'

'Good thing I do. And I'm a good teacher.'

'Really?' She arched an eyebrow. 'We never danced before.'

He stopped mid-step and dropped his arms. 'We were too busy doing other things, I suppose.'

Eleanor's cheeks heated and she was grateful for the shadowy dimness of the hallway. Why had she mentioned the past? Why had she referred to anything about their old relationship, their old selves?

'One dance, Eleanor.'

He made it sound like a challenge. And it *was* a challenge; suddenly Eleanor wanted to show Jace Zervas that she could dance with him and remain unaffected. She could walk away. She was desperate to prove to him—and to herself—that he really didn't affect or matter to her at all. And she'd enjoy it at the same time. One dance.

'Fine.'

She walked past him, stiff with resolution, back out into the crowded light of the party. She heard Jace walk behind her, felt the heat of his hand on the small of her back. The band she'd chosen herself was playing a lively swing tune and all around her couples were happily cutting up the floor. Eleanor wasn't much of a dancer—she was usually working behind the scenes, not *in* them—but she thought she could manage a brisk shuffle.

Jace's hand pressed against her back, steering her through the crowd to a spare space on the dance floor. Eleanor turned to face him, firm smile in place. Jace smiled lazily back—as if he knew exactly what she was thinking, that she was simply trying to prove something. Just as he was.

'Shall we?' Eleanor asked brightly and Jace reached for her hand, his fingers threading through hers.

'Oh, yes.'

He pulled her to him, and when Eleanor resisted that sensual tug he murmured so only she could hear, 'Come on, Eleanor. We're dancing.'

'Right.' She let him draw her closer, knowing it was dangerous, feeling that awful desire leap in her belly as she inhaled the woodsy musk of his cologne.

'You're dancing like a twelve-year-old boy,' he chided as Eleanor started an awkward box-step. 'And you're leading.'

'I can't help it,' Eleanor said, laughing reluctantly.

Jace placed his hand on her waist, his fingers splayed across her hip, and drew her close enough so she could feel the heat of him. 'This is how you do it,' he said mock sternly, and began to move her around the dance floor in a lively jitterbug.

Eleanor wasn't sure how she did it. Somehow Jace put enough pressure on her waist to guide her along, twisting and whirling her with such a natural ease that Eleanor was left breathless, amazed at her own gracefulness.

The other dancers had cleared a space around them, and several couples had stopped to watch, clapping their hands in time to the music.

'You're making a scene,' Eleanor hissed when she came close enough to Jace to have him hear. His arm slid along the length of hers before he grabbed her hand and whirled her in a neat, fast circle so her dress spun out around her in a silver arc.

'Isn't that the point?' he challenged with a wicked smile, and Eleanor felt her insides melt.

This was so dangerous. This was the Jace she'd once known, the Jace she'd fallen in love with. The Jace who had broken her heart. She preferred the harsh, hard man she'd met in her office; there had been no danger of falling in love with *him*.

'Where did you learn to dance?' she asked breathlessly as Jace spun her around yet again.

'I have five older sisters. How could I not learn how to dance?'

'Five?' she repeated in surprise. She'd had no idea.

'Now for the finale,' Jace said and Eleanor stiffened in alarm.

'I can't—'

'Yes,' he told her as he pulled her closer, 'you can.'

And before Eleanor knew what he was doing he'd flipped her right over so her legs had gone over her head until she was on her feet again, dazed and incredulous. Around them people clapped and cheered.

'*Jace!*'

'Wasn't that fun?'

'That doesn't matter—' she blustered. How many people had seen her underwear?

'Don't worry,' he murmured, drawing her close again, 'no one saw anything.'

'How did you—' She didn't finish that question and shook her head. It *had* been fun, yet she couldn't quite keep herself from still acting annoyed and defensive; those postures were her armour. They kept her safe. She wasn't ready to unbend entirely.

The song had ended, replaced by a slow jazz number. Distantly Eleanor recognised the sexy, mournful wail of a single saxophone as Jace lazily pulled her even closer so their hips collided and his hands slid down to her lower back, his fingers splayed across the curve of her bottom.

'Jace—' Eleanor hissed, trying to move out of the all-too-close contact. Around them couples swayed to the music.

'Relax. It's a slow dance.'

Relax? How on earth was she supposed to relax with her body pressed against Jace's, his hands moving lazily up and down her spine? She was conscious of how thin her dress was, how little separated their bodies—

Eleanor clamped down on that thought. Fine. She could endure this. She could still walk away with her head held high—except, there was no *enduring* about it. It was far, far too pleasant to let her body relax into Jace's, to enjoy the feel of his hand on her back, his fingers burning her through the thin material of her dress. Too wonderful to let him pull her closer, to lean her head against his chest so her lips hovered less than an inch from the warm skin of his neck.

They'd never danced before. There had been no opportunities. Their love affair had been conducted in the café where she'd worked, walks in the park, and the big double bed in Jace's apartment. Eleanor hadn't even known Jace could dance just as she hadn't known he had five older sisters. He'd never told her, just as he'd never told her so many things. She'd been in love with him, yet in some ways she'd barely known him. It made her wonder if you even could be in love with someone you hardly knew. Had it simply been infatuation?

'See how easy this is?' Jace murmured. His lips brushed her hair and his breath tickled her cheek. Eleanor closed her eyes.

Yes, it was easy. Far, far too easy. She'd wanted to cling to the knowledge that they were two different people now, that even if she could forgive and forget what had happened between them—which she didn't even know if she could—a relationship was impossible. Unwanted on both sides.

Yet in Jace's arms all those resolutions fell away, as insubstantial as smoke, or the snow that had already started to melt into slushy puddles. In Jace's arms, she was conscious only of how everything felt so wonderfully, painfully the same.

The song ended and they remained swaying for a heartbeat before Eleanor found the strength to break away. Her face was flushed and she could feel a rather large strand of hair against her cheek, falling down from her professional, sleek chignon. Her image was falling apart. *She* was falling apart.

'I need to go. There are things to do.'

'Okay.' She risked looking up, saw how shuttered Jace's eyes looked, his jaw taut. This dance had cost him something too. Why were they doing this? Flirting with the past? Flirting with each other? Surely it could only lead to heartache…for both of them.

'Thank you for the dance,' she said, and hurried away without waiting for Jace's reply.

Jace watched Eleanor weave her way through the crowd. His body tingled where he'd touched her. He felt alive, more alive than he had in years, and yet restless and edgy as well.

What was he doing? What was he trying to prove? Dancing with Eleanor was dangerous. There could be nothing for them now, not with the past still lying so heavily between them. Not when he was leaving in less than a week. He didn't even *want* there to be anything between them; he wasn't interested in love, and learning he might actually be fertile couldn't change that.

Could it?

The best thing—the wisest and safest—would be to leave Eleanor alone. To walk away right now, and let them both get on with their lives. Yet even as he made this resolution, Jace realised he was still looking for her. Waiting for her.

Wanting her.

* * *

Eleanor avoided Jace for the rest of the night, feeling ridiculous as she skulked in the corners of rooms, hurried down hallways, and kept an eagle eye out for his appearance. Yet avoiding Jace had become necessary for her sanity, her safety. That dance had broken down the barriers she'd erected between them, barriers between the past and the present. Barriers she needed. She didn't want to get close to Jace, couldn't let herself love him or be infatuated with him. Whatever it was—had been—she had no desire to feel it again. Not with a man she still couldn't trust. Not with Jace.

Still, she couldn't avoid him for ever. He found her after the party had finished, the last guests trickling out into the night, and the staff starting to clear the party's debris.

'Always busy,' he murmured.

Eleanor didn't turn around, though she could feel him behind her. 'I have a lot to do. It's a party to you, Jace, but for me it's work.'

He propped one shoulder against the wall of the Lake Room where she'd been going over her list of rented equipment on one of the cleared tables. 'It was a great party. And great work.'

'Thank you.' Needlessly she ticked an item off on her list. One of the staff hoisted a tray of dirty wine glasses and left the room, making Eleanor tinglingly aware of how alone she and Jace were. The last guests had gone into the park and the darkness, and, now that the room was cleared, all the staff seemed to have vanished. She ticked another item off on her list, eyes fixed firmly upon it.

'I'm leaving for Greece in three days,' he said quietly. He sounded sad. Eleanor tensed.

'I see.'

'I'd like to think…' He paused, clearing his throat. Eleanor looked up, surprised by the naked vulnerability in Jace's eyes. The list fell from her hand, forgotten. 'I'd like,' Jace started again, 'to return home knowing things are—resolved—between us.'

Resolved. The word echoed through her. What did that mean? How did you find resolution, that oft-touted closure? Eleanor wished she knew. 'Fine,' she said after a moment. 'Consider us resolved.' She picked up her list again and stared at it blindly.

'Eleanor—'

'I don't know what you want, Jace. Whatever it is, I don't think I can give it to you.' She swallowed, stared at her list. 'I'm sorry.' She might have danced with him, had even *wanted* to dance with him, but it meant nothing. She knew that, she felt it now. Her body might betray her again and again, but her mind and heart remembered just what Jace had done. Her mind and heart wouldn't forget. Couldn't forgive. She slipped her list into her bag and met Jace's troubled gaze. Even now her body reacted to his nearness, both with wanting and remembrance. Even now she remembered how she'd felt in his arms, both an hour ago and a lifetime ago. From somewhere she summoned the strength to move past him, making sure they didn't even brush shoulders. 'Goodnight, Jace.'

She walked out of the room without looking back, fumbling for her coat by the front door. She usually stayed for longer after a party, making absolutely sure everything was cleaned up and taken care of. But she couldn't tonight, couldn't handle another moment of being near Jace, of enduring the temptation of being near him.

She hated that her body was so weak, that she still desired the man who had betrayed her. At least she'd been strong enough to walk away.

Jace stood alone in the Lake Room, everything empty and silent around him. In the distance he heard the door click open and shut. Eleanor had gone.

He let out a long, slow breath. It was better this way. It really was. It had to be. Yet even so, the restlessness didn't leave him; the regret still weighed heavily on his heart.

It might be better this way, but it didn't feel like it. Too many things still lay between them, words unspoken that needed to be said.

Consider us resolved.

He didn't.

His body taut with grim purpose, Jace strode from the room.

Outside the park was dark, the last guests already long gone. Eleanor dug her hands deep into the pockets of her coat and walked resolutely towards Fifth Avenue. There should be plenty of cabs there, even at this hour.

She'd only been walking a few minutes, skirting the edge of the Sailboat Pond, afloat with model boats in the spring and summer but now drained and empty, when she heard footsteps behind her. Eleanor's heart stilled even as she quickened her pace. The park was generally safe at night these days, but this was New York and she knew to be careful.

'Eleanor, I'm sorry.'

It was Jace. Eleanor's heart resumed its normal thump for only a second before it began beating all the faster. It was *Jace*. She slowed her pace and turned around.

'What did you say?'

'I'm sorry.' She could barely see him in the darkness; the only light was from a high, thin crescent of moon just emerging from behind the clouds. She couldn't make out the expression on his face, but she could hear the contrition and regret tearing his voice and it startled her.

She hitched her bag higher up on her shoulder. 'What for?'

'For hurting you so badly.' Jace took a step closer to her, and now the moon cast a pale, silvery glow over his features, etched in regret. Eleanor's breath dried in her throat. 'For walking away so utterly. For not being there when you must have been going through a very difficult time.'

'Don't—' Eleanor whispered. He had no idea just how difficult a time she'd been through. He had no idea how much she'd needed to hear these words, and yet how afraid she was to hear them, because an apology required a response. It meant things would change. *She* would have to change.

'Don't say sorry?' Jace smiled, that wonderful crooked smile Eleanor knew and had once loved. 'But I have to. For my sake, as well as your own. We can't be—resolved—until I say it. I know that.'

'I don't need—' Eleanor began, roughly, for her throat was already clogged and tight. Yet she couldn't even finish the sentence. It was a lie. She *did* need. She needed Jace to apologise. She needed to be able to forgive him. For ten years she'd managed to move on without it, but her heart had stayed in the same place. She hadn't realised just how much until Jace had come back into her life.

He was right in front of her now, so close she could reach out and touch him if she wanted to. She didn't move. 'Will you forgive me, Eleanor?' Jace asked softly. 'For hurting you so much?'

Eleanor wanted to shake her head. She wanted to cry. She wanted to tell him she wouldn't, because she was still angry and hurt and afraid, and yet she wanted to say she would because she needed the closure, the redemption. She nodded jerkily, unable to offer him more.

It didn't matter. Jace closed the small space between them, pulling her into his arms. She felt the soft wool of his coat against her cold cheek as she remained in the circle of his embrace, unresisting, unable to move or push away as she surely should do. 'I'm sorry,' he said again, his voice rough with emotion, and the shell around Eleanor's hardened heart finally cracked and broke.

'I forgive you,' she whispered, the words barely more than a breath of sound. Her throat was so tight. She tilted her head up to look at him, meaning only to offer absolution, yet there must have been too much yearning in her eyes—too much desire—for Jace's own expression darkened and after a second's hesitation—a second that seemed to last for ever—he lowered his mouth to hers.

The first brush of his lips against hers was a shock,

electrifying her from the tips of her fingers to the very centre of her soul.

Then her senses sweetly sang to life as both body and mind and even heart remembered this, remembered Jace. How he felt. How he tasted. How right she'd always been in his arms and under his touch.

Her lips yielded to his, parting, inviting, and Jace took full advantage, deepening the kiss so Eleanor felt that plunging sensation of helpless desire deep in her belly, so she craved more, and *more*, her hands sliding over his coat, across his shoulders, down his back, bringing her closer to him.

She didn't know how long the kiss went on. And it was more than a kiss. Jace's hands had slipped under her coat, under her dress, cold against her skin and yet still enflaming her with his touch so that both their breathing was ragged and Eleanor's mind was as hazy and high as a cloud.

Her head dropped back, her back arching, a moan escaping her lips as his hands roved over her body and his mouth moved on hers. It had been so long. It had been ten years.

She couldn't think past this moment, couldn't register anything but the onslaught of her senses…until she heard two teenagers' raucous laughter from across the pond, the ugly sound jolting her out of that desire-induced haze and right out of Jace's arms. She jerked away, her chest rising and falling in shock, in shame, while she stared at him with dazed, disbelieving eyes. He looked back at her, his expression just as stunned. Neither of them spoke.

Eleanor could hardly believe what she'd just allowed. What she'd done. He said sorry and she melted into his arms? She'd practically begged him to touch her, *take* her? Jace looked as if he hadn't even meant to kiss her, and maybe he hadn't. Maybe she'd kissed him without realising—

'Eleanor—'

'No.' She couldn't hear what he was going to say, no matter what it was. Anything Jace said now was sure to break her. 'This shouldn't have happened.'

'I know.' Those two sorry words almost made her cry.

Somehow she didn't want him to admit it was a mistake, even though she knew it was. 'Even so—'

'No,' Eleanor said again. There was no *even so*. There couldn't be. She shook her head, backing away, and then with a stifled cry she fled into the night.

Jace watched Eleanor run through the darkness as if the very demons of hell were on her heels. Perhaps she felt they were. She had clearly been shocked by that kiss, and frankly so had he.

He'd meant only to say sorry, to make up for the past, and instead he'd reopened it, ripped the scabs off their scars. His heart ached with remembered pain. His body ached with unfulfilled desire.

What was he doing? Why couldn't he just leave Eleanor Langley alone? Jace realised he was still walking towards Fifth Avenue, following her fleeing footsteps. He slowed his stride.

Ever since Eleanor had come back into his life—ever since he'd discovered she'd been telling the truth—he hadn't been able to stop thinking of her. Thinking about the what ifs, wondering if life could give them a second chance.

Jace stopped in his tracks. A second chance at what? At *love*?

Did he really want that?

The last ten years he'd been hardening his heart against love, against any messy emotion. He'd focused on his business, building an empire instead of a dynasty.

And yet now…now he wanted more. He wanted Eleanor.

Ellie.

He wanted to reawaken the woman he'd lost when he'd walked out ten years ago. He wanted Ellie to find herself again, her true self, the self whom he'd loved and who had loved him. He wasn't even sure why; he didn't know what he even wanted with that woman. He'd lost her once, and he'd spent the intervening years making sure he never lost—anything or anyone—again.

Did he really want that change? That risk?

Did Ellie?

And how the hell could any of it happen, when he was leaving in a few days?

Jace stopped walking. The past was better buried. He knew that, felt it. No matter how these if onlys and what ifs might torment him, he knew they were only that. Possibilities, not realities. Not even hopes.

Distantly he heard the teenagers move off, still laughing raucously, and the laboured chug of the Fifth Avenue bus as it headed downtown. Letting out a long, slow breath, Jace slowly turned around and walked in the other direction.

CHAPTER SIX

ELEANOR didn't go back to her apartment. She didn't want to be alone, so she took a cab to the West Village, where her best friend Allie had a studio on the top floor of a brownstone. They'd both been interns at Premier Planning nine years ago. Allie had lasted two weeks. Eleanor had stayed for ever.

Even though it was now after midnight, she knew she could trust Allie to welcome her with open arms—and an open heart.

Still, she had to press the buzzer for a good thirty seconds before Allie came to the intercom.

'Who is it?' she demanded in a voice that sounded both sleepy and irritated.

Too emotional and fragile to explain, Eleanor just said, 'Me.'

Allie pressed the buzzer.

She was waiting outside the door in her pyjamas, hugging herself in the cold of the corridor, as Eleanor made her way up the six narrow flights of stairs.

'Eleanor, what on earth happened? You look terrible.'

'Thanks,' Eleanor managed wryly, and Allie shrugged this aside, taking in Eleanor's up-do and silvery dress.

'Actually, you look fantastic. You *sound* terrible. What's wrong?'

'Everything, it feels like,' Eleanor replied, her words wobbly. Now that she was finally here with Allie, safe, loved, the reality of her confrontation with Jace—and that wonderful, awful, confusing kiss—was slamming into her, leaving her more than shaken. Leaving her shattered.

Allie ushered her inside the cosy apartment, plonking the kettle on the stove before Eleanor had even asked.

'You want to talk about it? Didn't you have an event tonight?'

Eleanor sank onto the worn futon and kicked off her heels, nodding wearily. Allie's apartment was so different from her own modishly sterile condo; it was colourful and cluttered and shabby, and Eleanor loved it. Now it made her ache just a little bit for the kind of apartment she'd once had, the kind of life she'd once had. The kind of person she'd once been.

You're the kind of person you never wanted to be.

Eleanor pushed the thought away. Allie sank onto the futon across from Eleanor, flicked her long braid over one shoulder and propped her chin on her fist. 'So?'

'He came back.'

Allie's eyes widened, her breath coming out in a slow hiss. Eleanor knew she didn't need to explain who *he* was. One night long ago, when they'd both had too much wine, she'd told Allie her whole sordid story. Or most of it, anyway. She'd left out some of the heartache, the consuming loss that was too private to share.

'He did?' Allie finally said. 'How—?'

Eleanor didn't want to explain it. She didn't have the strength or will. 'Party,' she said simply, and Allie nodded. It was enough.

'What happened? Did the bastard finally apologise, I hope?'

Eleanor let out a choked laugh. 'Yes,' she managed, and covered her face with her hands.

'And isn't that a good thing?' Allie asked cautiously. Eleanor was prevented from answering by the shrill whistle of the kettle. Allie got up to make their tea, and Eleanor sagged against the futon. It *was* a good thing. At least, she'd always thought it would be. Yet when someone asked for forgiveness, you were meant to give it; you were meant to let go. And Eleanor wasn't sure she could. She might have told Jace she forgave him, but those were only words. *Could* she forgive him? What would happen if she did?

Allie returned, handing Eleanor a mug of tea before settling back onto the futon. 'So it doesn't seem like a good thing,' she remarked wryly. 'Why not?'

Eleanor let out a hiccuppy laugh. 'Well, I suppose it's not so much the apology, as the kiss that came after it.'

There was a second's silence and then Allie nodded. 'Ah.' She took a sip of tea. 'Was it nice?'

Eleanor burst out laughing, nearly spluttering her tea. It felt good to laugh, despite the pain and regret still tearing at her. 'That was the last thing I expected you to say.'

Allie shrugged. 'For all the apparent heartache it's causing you, I hope it was.'

'Very nice,' Eleanor admitted after a moment. She gazed down into the milky depths of her tea. 'Very nice,' she repeated quietly. Even now she could remember how good Jace had felt, how *right*, which was ridiculous because there had been nothing right about it all. It had been very, very wrong.

'So why exactly did he kiss you?' Allie asked after a moment. She tucked her knees up to her chest and looked at Eleanor over the rim of her mug. 'Was he just caught up in the moment?'

'I don't know,' Eleanor said slowly. Why *had* Jace kissed her? Had it been a spontaneous gesture, as Allie had said? He had seemed so surprised, as stunned as she had…yet she could hardly believe that Jace would be so out of control. Had he been proving to her that she was still attracted to him? Had it been a mere amusement? Or worse—far worse—a *pity* kiss?

'Eleanor, stop whatever you're thinking. You're looking way too freaked out.'

Eleanor groaned. 'I'm feeling freaked out. You know I haven't had much time—or inclination—for relationships, Allie. I can't *do* this—'

'Does he want a relationship?'

Eleanor groaned again. 'No, of course not. That is—I don't think so. I shouldn't even care.'

'But you do,' Allie filled in quietly and Eleanor bit her lip, nipping hard.

'No,' she finally said, firmly. 'I don't. I can't. Ten years ago he broke my heart and—more than that.' She twisted the mug, her tea barely touched, around in her hands. 'My whole life collapsed, Allie. Everything. I never told you how—how bad it was, but it was. Bad.' She tried to smile wryly, but her lips trembled instead. 'Really bad.'

'Oh, Eleanor.' Allie reached over to place a hand on top of hers. 'I'm sorry.'

'So am I. And that's why this kiss—for whatever reason—was a bad idea. I'm not going to ever let myself feel that way again. Be used that way. And,' Eleanor finished, her voice turning hard and flinty, 'the simple fact is, I may have changed a lot in ten years, but Jace Zervas hasn't.' Not enough. Not in ways that mattered. She smiled grimly at her friend. 'I don't think he's changed at all.'

Eleanor spent the night on Allie's futon, and slept deeply and dreamlessly. By the time she swam to consciousness the next morning, the sun was high in the sky and Allie had already gone out for the coffee and croissants.

'I feel like I've been hit by a truck,' Eleanor muttered as she pushed her hair out of her face and blinked in the sunlight flooding the room. She hadn't even washed her face before going to bed, and her eyes felt sticky both with sleep and dried mascara.

'You basically were,' Allie replied cheerfully. 'The Jace Zervas Express.' She handed Eleanor a paper cup of coffee and a flaky croissant. 'Here. Sustenance.'

'You're amazing.'

Allie grinned. 'I know.'

Eleanor sat cross-legged on the sofa and ate the buttery croissant, licking the crumbs from her fingers, before she started on her coffee. She hadn't eaten much last night, as busy as she'd been with the details of the party, and she was starving.

Her cellphone beeped just as she took her first sip of coffee.

'My boss,' she explained when she'd located the phone and listened to Lily's brief message. She sounded her usual terse self, and simply asked her to call, which made Eleanor feel a flutter of panic. Had Jace talked to Lily? Had the party *not* been a success after all?

Had that kiss changed everything?

She ended the message and dropped her cellphone back into her bag. Leaning back against the sofa she took a sip of coffee, determined to forget Lily, forget Jace, forget everything, if just for a day. It was Saturday; she was with Allie. And she needed a break. She turned to Allie, smiling with bright determination. 'Let's go out. Do something fun. Go to the Greenmarket in Union Square and buy funky jewellery at St Mark's Place.'

'Funky jewellery?' Allie repeated, eyebrows arched. 'When have you ever worn funky jewellery?'

Eleanor bit her lip, her smile wobbling just a little bit. She used to wear funky jewellery. She used to look and feel and *be* so different.

She simply wasn't that person any more, and she didn't think she ever could be again. After she'd lost both Jace and their baby, she'd ruthlessly gone about becoming someone else…the person she was now.

The kind of person you never wanted to be.

Shrugging away the sorrow this thought caused, she smiled once more at Allie. 'Well, let's go to a museum, then. The Met or the MOMA.' She took her last sip of coffee, her voice taking on an edge. 'You're right, I'm really not a funky jewellery kind of person.'

Monday morning came soon enough, and as Eleanor walked through Premier Planning's office she was uncomfortably aware of the curious looks of everyone on the office floor, the sideways glances, the open speculation. Her skin prickled. What had happened? What had Jace done?

Then she stopped in the doorway of her office, for there in the centre of her desk was the most enormous, most outrageous bouquet of flowers she'd ever seen. She dropped her bag on the floor and approached the arrangement of creamy white lilies and small, violet blooms that a card tucked in among the leaves told her was glory-of-the-snow.

Snow.

Her heart constricted. A little envelope had been taped to the crystal vase, and Eleanor took it with trembling fingers. She slipped the stiff white card out and read the two words printed on it: *Sorry. Again.*

Her fingers clenched on the card. Sorry for what? Sorry for the kiss? Sorry for—

'Well, well.'

Eleanor turned around, the card still clutched in her fingers. Lily stood in the doorway, as sharp and freshly pressed as ever, the expression on her thin face impossible to read.

'Good morning, Lily.'

'I'd say from those flowers that Zervas was pleased with the party.'

'I hope so.'

'I know he was pleased because he called me Saturday morning to tell me so. I knew we could do it,' Lily told her in a smug voice that made Eleanor wonder if her boss was taking credit for pulling off the event.

'That's…wonderful?' she said numbly.

Lily narrowed her eyes. 'It is, isn't it? You don't sound too thrilled, though. And you look terrible.'

Leave it to Lily not to sugarcoat it, Eleanor thought sourly. She moved the flowers to a side table. 'I'm just exhausted. Organising a party like that in just a week takes it out of even me.'

'You're right,' Lily conceded grudgingly. 'You can take a half-day, if you like.'

Eleanor shook her head. She didn't need more time to think, to dwell, to wonder. Nor did she need people like Jill or Laura eager to keep her clients or steal more while she was away. She needed to be here, at work, where she was needed and useful and busy. 'No, thanks. I'm fine. I need to catch up on all my other accounts anyway.'

Yet even as Eleanor worked solidly throughout the day, she found it still gave her mind plenty of time to wonder. To remember. She relived every second of that kiss with Jace, how unbearably good it had felt to be held by him again. How she realised her body had been waiting to be held again—by him—for ten long years.

How infuriated and frustrated and *scared* it made her feel. She didn't want to want him.

She was just about to leave for the day when her phone rang. Thinking it was a callback from a client, she reached for the phone quickly, her voice brisk and professional.

'Eleanor Langley.'

'Hello, Ellie.' A pause, and she heard a wry note of laughter in his voice as he corrected himself. 'Sorry. Eleanor.'

Her fingers clenched on the phone. Blood drained from her face, raced to other parts of her body. 'Hello, Jace.'

'I'm leaving for Greece tomorrow.' He spoke quietly, almost sadly. 'I just wanted to say I'm sorry. For the other night. I know me kissing you wasn't on either of our agendas.'

Agendas. She pictured herself pencilling in *kiss Jace.* No, that had definitely not been on her agenda. And obviously not on Jace's either, Eleanor acknowledged bleakly. 'The flowers did the job admirably,' she said after a moment, her voice sounding constricted.

'I'm glad you liked them.'

Eleanor didn't answer, couldn't, because her throat had tightened so terribly. The silence ticked on between them, punctuated only by the soft sound of their breathing.

Finally Jace spoke again. 'So I suppose this is goodbye. I don't intend to return to New York.'

'Not even to manage Atrikides Holdings?'

'I've appointed a CEO,' Jace said. 'Leandro Atrikides's nephew. That was the plan all along.'

'Whose plan?'

'Leandro's.' He sounded weary, and Eleanor realised with a jolt that the corporate takeover might not have been quite as ruthless as she'd thought. *Jace* wasn't as ruthless as she had thought.

But it didn't matter, because he was leaving New York. And there could be—would be—nothing between them anyway, which was how she wanted it. How it had to be. The past could be forgiven, maybe, but not forgotten. Not undone.

'I see,' she managed. Her voice sounded distant and polite despite the ache in her throat and even in her heart. 'Well, goodbye, then.'

Jace was silent, long enough for Eleanor to wonder what he was thinking. What he wanted to say. What *she* wanted him to say.

'Goodbye, Eleanor,' he said, and then he put down the phone.

Staring into space, Eleanor realised that Jace had just left her a second time. At least this time he'd said goodbye.

Jace stood up and walked over to the floor-to-ceiling window of Leandro Atrikides's office, the view of Central Park now shrouded in shadows.

Tomorrow morning he'd take his private jet back to Athens. He had plenty of work to keep him busy, meetings to attend, companies to control, decisions to make. A life.

Yet right now it all felt empty, meaningless, and all he could think of was the woman he'd left, the woman he was leaving again. The life he'd lost a decade ago.

Irritated, Jace shook off his maudlin thoughts. They were not worthy of him. Regret was a useless emotion. The best option, the only option, was to move on. To forget. As they both surely should do.

And that was what he *wanted* to do, anyway. He wasn't interested in resurrecting some youthful affair that had most likely been doomed from the start. He wasn't interested in becoming that carefree young man again, the man with a heart to break, even if he grieved the loss of the woman he'd once known. He'd wanted to bring that woman back last night; he thought apologising would help. Kissing her wouldn't. Didn't.

That kiss, Jace knew, had been a mistake. Even if it hadn't felt like one at the time.

That kiss had unearthed memories, desire, regrets—all of which Jace wanted to keep buried, and he had no doubt that Eleanor did too.

Sighing, shrugging off these thoughts, he told himself he should return to his penthouse hotel suite. He'd order in and go to bed early, take a morning flight back to Athens. He was neither needed nor wanted here.

Yet still he remained, hands in his pockets, staring out at a darkening sky.

Three months later

'Why do you work so hard?'

Jace looked up from the financial newspaper he'd been scanning as he drank his morning coffee. 'Sorry,' he said, giving his sister Alecia a still-distracted smile. 'Habit.' He reached for one of the rolls on the table. They were sitting in one of the cafés off Kolonaki Square, in one of Athens's best neighborhoods.

Across from him Alecia made a face and reached for a roll herself. 'I don't mean reading your newspaper, Jace. It's everything. Ever since you came back from that trip you've been like a grumpy bear, growling at everyone who sees you. And you've missed three family dinners—that's at least two too many. I know you try to miss them anyway, but still...' She smiled teasingly as she said it, but even Jace could see the shadows of worry in her eyes.

He broke his roll in half. 'What trip do you mean?'

'The one to the States. New York, wasn't it?'

Jace shouldn't have asked. He already knew what trip, knew what lay behind his sister's concerned comments.

Eleanor. He couldn't get her out of his mind. He hadn't been the same since he'd seen her. Since he'd left her. Again.

Sighing, he reached for his cup and took a small sip of the strong, syrupy Greek coffee.

'I'm worried about you, you know.'

'Don't be.' The words came out harshly, too harshly, for he and Alecia had always enjoyed a close relationship. She was older than him by only eighteen months, and the only one of his sisters still to be unmarried. She understood him perhaps better than anyone else did, and she was the only person he'd told about Ellie. Yet he hadn't told her about Eleanor, or what had happened in New York three months ago.

'Jace? What's going on?'

'Nothing.' His throat constricted and his fingers tightened around the coffee cup. He wasn't ready to share everything he'd learned in New York: that he'd made a mistake, that he wasn't infertile, that he'd ruined what might have been his only chance at happiness and perhaps even love. He could barely voice those sentiments to himself. For the last three months he'd been working as hard as he could to keep from thinking about them. To keep from thinking about anything.

Yet it obviously hadn't worked, for Alecia had seen that something was amiss, and Eleanor never really left his thoughts. She invaded his dreams. He felt her like a constant presence, a mist over his mind, even though she was thousands of miles away.

'Is it a woman?' Alecia asked playfully, and Jace's head jerked up.

'What?'

'A woman.' Alecia smiled, her chin resting on her laced

fingers. 'If I didn't know you better, I'd think it was a woman. You seem almost lovesick.'

Lovesick. What a terrible expression. Love. *Sick*. And he didn't love Eleanor; he didn't even know her any more.

'Alecia, that's ridiculous.'

'Is it?' Alecia cocked her head. 'I know you haven't given any women a chance since that conniving slut back in Boston—'

'Don't.' Jace bit the word off, heard the tension and anger in his voice. Alecia blinked in surprise. 'I don't want to talk about her.'

'I know how much she hurt you, Jace. Even if you've never wanted to admit it.'

'Don't,' he said again, and barely managed to get the word out. He turned his head, not wanting Alecia to see the naked emotion and pain on his face. Not wanting to feel it himself. He missed her, he knew. He couldn't hide from it. He missed Ellie. *Eleanor*. Since seeing her in New York, he hadn't felt complete or whole or happy.

He *needed* her.

He just didn't want to.

'All right, then,' she said after a moment. 'Let's talk about something else. Papa is going to be seventy next month, and no one's done a thing about it.'

Jace tensed, as he always did when his father was mentioned, but then he made himself relax. 'And what,' he asked Alecia with a bland smile, 'are we supposed to do about it exactly?'

'A party, Jace! I know Elana usually organises such things, but she's busy with her four—Lukas is applying to university this year—and Tabitha is pregnant with her third—'

'Her third?' Jace murmured. 'Already?' He could never keep track of his sisters and their growing brood. Admittedly, he didn't try very hard. He sent expensive presents and occasionally he showed up. For so long he'd felt separate from all of them, with their busy lives and their bands of children. He'd felt so *other*.

Yet now he didn't need to; he'd gone to a fertility specialist as soon as he'd returned to Athens, and the results had come back two weeks ago. He had, the doctor told him, limited fertility. It would still be possible to have a child; it would have been possible ten years ago.

It had been. He thought of the daughter he'd had and never known, and then closed his mind off from the memory-that-wasn't.

He'd avoided thinking about the implications of the doctor's news because it hurt too much. It hurt to realise he had wasted so many years of his life; it hurt even to think how glad his father would be at the news now. His existence would finally be validated. Jace hadn't told him—or anyone—yet. It wasn't as if he were about to run off and make that oh-so needed heir. Unlike his father, he had no desperate urge to create a dynasty. He refused to be defined by either his inability or ability to have children.

'Jace, are you listening to a word I'm saying?' Alecia asked, good-natured impatience edging her voice, and Jace smiled in apology.

'Sorry. Go on. Tabitha's pregnant and Elana's busy.'

'And Kaitrona is hopeless at organising these things, and Parthenope isn't speaking to Papa—'

'Parthenope isn't? Why not?'

Alecia waved a hand in dismissal. 'Oh, who knows? Someone's always in an argument with him. He said something rude to Christos once—'

'Ah.' Christos was Parthenope's husband, a charming city type that his father didn't trust. And, Jace knew well, his father had always been a plain speaker.

You're sterile. You cannot have children. What use is it to me, to have no more Zervas men to follow me? What good are you?

'What about you, then?' he asked, pouring them both more coffee.

'I just started a new job and it has crazy hours,' Alecia replied. 'Which you'd know, if you listened to me for more than five minutes. Honestly, Jace, you're hopeless. Who is she?'

'*She* is no one,' Jace replied, an edge to his voice. 'Don't start assuming things and spreading rumours, Alecia.'

'Who, me?' She blinked innocently. 'Anyway, since none of us can do it, that only leaves one person.'

'Mother?' Jace guessed, and Alecia rolled her eyes.

'You, Jace, you! You can organise a party. I thought we could have it out on that island villa of yours. You hardly ever go there, and it's the most amazing place I've ever seen.'

Jace stilled, his face blanking. Give his father a party? A celebration thrown by the son who had been nothing but a disappointment? Such a party could only be an insult, a mockery, especially considering how strained and distant their relationship had been and still was. 'I don't think that's a good idea, Alecia.'

'I know you and Papa have your differences, Jace, but you're his son—'

'I'm not the right person to do this,' Jace cut her off flatly. He knew his sisters didn't understand the tension between him and his father; Aristo Zervas had wanted to keep his son's infertility—his family's shame—a secret.

'Fine, then hire someone to do it,' Alecia replied. A steely look that Jace knew well had entered her eye. She wasn't going to let go of this.

'Alecia—' He stopped as her suggestion sank in. *Hire someone to do it.* The words echoed in Jace's mind, reverberated in his heart. He felt, bizarrely, as if everything had just slid into place. As if everything suddenly made sense. It was as if he'd been waiting for this opportunity, and now that it had fallen into his lap he knew just what to do. What he wanted to do, what he needed to do.

'So?' Alecia asked, sipping her coffee, her smile turning just a little bit smug. 'What do you think?'

'I think,' Jace said slowly, 'that it's a good idea. And I know just the person to do it.'

* * *

Eleanor picked up another stone, worn silky smooth by the endless tide, and, aiming carefully, threw it into the Long Island Sound. Satisfied, she watched it skip four times before sinking beneath the waves. She heard the crunch of footsteps on the sand behind her.

'You've been doing that for hours.'

Eleanor reached for another stone, offering her mother a quick smile. 'It's therapeutic.'

'You need therapy?'

'I live in New York. Doesn't everyone there need it?'

'Probably.' Her mother sighed and sat down on the hard, cold sand. It was almost April, and, although the trees were starting to bud and daffodils lined the drive up to Heather Langley's beach cottage, the wind and waves were still cold. 'You want to tell me about it?' she asked eventually and Eleanor skipped another stone across the water. She'd arrived at her mother's place last night, and she'd leave tomorrow. They hadn't spoken much beyond pleasantries; her mother knew better than to press.

'Not particularly,' she replied lightly. She knew her mother—and her mother knew her—too well to dissemble or pretend there wasn't anything going on. Yet she didn't trust her mother with the truth.

Their relationship had always been a strained one, marred by ambition and yet marked with moments of intimacy and caring. Still, it wasn't enough to make her want now to unburden her heart and reveal her vulnerabilities.

'Lily says you're doing well at work. Amazing, really.'

'Thanks.' It seemed like the only thing in her life that *was* going right. Since Jace had left, she'd poured herself into work more than ever before. It grated on her nerves that her mother and her boss talked about her, checked up on her. It was ridiculous and even inappropriate, yet Eleanor knew she couldn't tell either of them that. They were best friends, competitors and colleagues until a minor heart attack had forced Heather into early retirement. She'd left her job and the city and taken this cottage out on Long Island. Once in a while she planned someone's beach party in the Hamptons, but her career was essentially finished, and Eleanor thought it was the best thing that had ever happened to her mother—and to their relationship.

She sighed, sinking onto the sand next to her mother, her elbows resting on her knees. 'It's nothing, really. I'm just restless.'

'You've been at Premier Planning for a long time,' Heather said after a moment. 'Maybe you should think about something else.'

Eleanor rounded her eyes in mock horror. 'Give up my job? That's the last thing I'd expect you to say.'

Heather shrugged. 'A job doesn't have to be everything. I know it seemed like it was for me, but—' She stopped, uncertain, and Eleanor smiled to help her out.

'I know.'

Her mother smiled in apology. There was still so much that hadn't been said between them. From her fatherless childhood and her mother's workaholic schedule, to the whole mess of Jace and her pregnancy—an entire language of loss and hurt that neither of them knew how to speak.

'Well,' Heather said finally, 'a sabbatical maybe.'

Eleanor shook her head. 'I'm okay.' She couldn't give up work; it was all she had. Yet she didn't know *what* she wanted to do. Ever since Jace had left New York—ever since he'd kissed her—she'd been feeling restless and edgy and uncertain. Wanting something different. Something more. Maybe even wanting Jace. Yet she wasn't about to abandon her senses or her job for some impossible dream, some distant fantasy that was never meant to be real.

Smiling, she stood up and stretched her hand out to her mother. Heather took it. 'Come on. It's pretty cold out here. I've got one more afternoon before I have to head back to the city, and I fully intend to beat you at Scrabble for once.'

Laughing, Heather let her change the subject. 'I'd like to see you try.'

* * *

Monday morning came soon enough, and Eleanor arrived at work a bit weary from her three-hour journey on the Hampton Jitney the night before.

Shelley, the receptionist, rose from her desk as Eleanor entered the office. 'I have your nine o'clock waiting in your office.'

'My nine o'clock?' Eleanor repeated. She'd gone through her schedule that morning while sipping coffee at the sink, and her first appointment was at ten.

'Yes, he said he'd like to wait there.' Shelley, all of twenty-two years old, made a swoony type of face that caused Eleanor a ripple of unease.

'All right,' she murmured, walking down the hallway. Her office door, she saw, was closed. Lily poked her head out of her own office.

'I pencilled him in,' she told Eleanor briskly. 'Apparently he was *very* impressed. Would only have you for this project, and this time there's no rush.'

Eleanor's unease increased to foreboding as she reached for the knob of her door and turned.

'Hello, Eleanor.'

Jace Zervas stood in the centre of her office.

CHAPTER SEVEN

'WHAT are you doing here?'

Eleanor closed the door quickly behind her before her boss could hear any more of the conversation. Her heart was thudding heavily and her palms felt slick. Even more alarming were the sudden nerves that fluttered through her, making her tingle in—what? Annoyance? Anticipation? *Excitement?*

She sidestepped Jace to move behind her desk, where she felt safer. Slipping off her coat, she felt a flicker of gratitude that she was wearing one of her smarter outfits: a cream silk blouse and a cherry-red pencil skirt, with nails freshly manicured to match. Her hair was pulled up in a sleek twist, and her appearance felt like both her armour and her ammunition. She used it; she hid behind it.

'A party, of course.' He smiled, but Eleanor thought she saw a shadow of something in his eyes—uncertainty? Fear? This was foreign territory for both of them. He'd shed his cashmere trench coat and wore a charcoal-grey suit that matched his grey eyes perfectly. His silver-grey silk tie emphasised their metallic glints, and Eleanor had trouble tearing her gaze away from him.

'A party?' she repeated, looking down to reshuffle a few random papers on her desk. 'I hardly think I'm an appropriate candidate for—'

'You're the best.'

She looked up. 'I'm not that good.'

Jace took a step closer, one finger to his lips. 'Shh. Don't let Lily hear you.' He smiled, teasingly, and Eleanor felt those wretched nerves flutter through her again, as flighty and feather-brained as the pigeons crowding Central Park, fighting over a few paltry crumbs. 'She's quite a dragon,' Jace continued. 'She was business partners with your mother?' At Eleanor's sharp intake of breath he looked up and smiled. 'We had a little chat while I was waiting for you.'

'I really think it's better, Jace, if someone else organises this party. Anyway, I didn't think you were even coming back to New York.'

'This party's not in New York.'

Eleanor's breath came out in a rush. 'Then I'm certainly not the right person to plan it. Everything I've done is New-York-based—'

'You organised a birthday party in the Hamptons.'

'Still city-based,' Eleanor countered firmly. 'The client lived year round in Manhattan. Anyway, it's not worth arguing about. I don't care if your party is in Times Square, I don't want to organise it.' Brave words. Brave sentiments. She wished she sounded stronger. Felt surer. In truth she felt horribly uncertain. Half of her wanted to leap at the chance of spending more time with Jace; half of her wanted to run away.

The contradictory nature of her own emotions was ridiculous. And annoying.

'Actually,' Jace said, smiling faintly as he watched her, 'the party is in Greece. It's my father's seventieth birthday party.'

'What?' The word was more of a squawk. Jace's smile deepened so Eleanor saw his dimple. She wished she didn't. That dimple made him look friendly, approachable. Desirable.

'Have you ever been to Greece?' he asked as he started to stroll round her office, gazing at the rather pedestrian artwork on her walls.

'No,' she replied flatly. 'In fact, I've tried to avoid the whole country.'

'I think you would enjoy it. It's beautiful this time of year. Not too hot.'

'I'd hardly be relaxing,' Eleanor countered, then wished she hadn't. She didn't even want to discuss this. She was not going to Greece.

'Well, I don't want to run you ragged like last time,' Jace replied. 'The party's not for nearly a month.'

'Doesn't matter. I can't organise a party like that from here, and I can hardly go to Greece for a month.'

Jace stopped strolling and turned around to face her. He was smiling, but his face still looked grave. 'Can't you?' he asked softly.

Suddenly the atmosphere in the room changed, a different kind of tension tautening the air between them. Suddenly Jace seemed very close, even though he hadn't moved. Eleanor drew in a deep, shuddery breath.

'Don't, Jace.'

'Don't?' he repeated, the word a question, and Eleanor shook her head. She didn't want to explain. She didn't even know what to explain. She just knew that seeing him again was both a joy and agony, the emotions tangled so closely that she could not separate one from the other, or from herself. She wished he hadn't come, yet she'd been waiting for him to come.

He must have sensed something of her turmoil, for he took a step closer and said with a little smile, 'A couple of weeks in Greece. Can't you think of worse things?'

A couple of weeks in Greece *with you*, Eleanor amended silently. 'I can't leave my other clients for that long,' she began, trying to stay professional.

'Lily said someone else could take them. Laura or someone?'

Laura. Of course. She'd snagged her clients last time. Eleanor sagged into her chair as she felt the first flickers of defeat. 'You've already spoken to Lily,' she stated flatly and Jace shrugged.

'How could I not?'

She looked up, her eyes wide and meeting his own directly, daring him to be honest. 'Why me?'

'Why not you?' Jace countered quietly.

Eleanor swallowed, her gaze sliding away. 'You know why.'

Jace was silent for a moment, and when he spoke again his voice was light. 'I don't know any other event planners, and I think you're the best for the job.'

He didn't want to talk about the past. Fine, she didn't either, so she'd stick with the present. There was enough trouble with that. '*Me*? How about someone Greek for starters?' Eleanor drew in a breath, ready to launch into a tirade of how she couldn't go with Jace, she couldn't plan his party. She didn't want to. She was afraid to. She *wouldn't*.

'Actually, Eleanor, you'd be doing me a favour,' Jace cut her off, his voice quiet and a little sad. Eleanor closed her mouth with a surprised snap. 'My relationship with my father has never been—what it could be. What it should be.' He glanced away, his expression turning distant, shuttered. 'I'm afraid I've been a disappointment to my father, in many ways,' he confessed in a low voice. 'This party could help in healing our rift.'

This was more than Jace had ever shared with her before. About his life. About himself. She felt as if she'd been given a tiny glimpse into his mind, his heart, and it left her aching and curious and wanting to know more.

She cleared her throat, striving to keep her tone professional. 'I still don't know if I'm the right person for this, Jace…considering.' It occurred to her that perhaps he'd never told his family about her. Perhaps he'd walked right back into life in Greece without a single backward glance or thought at all. Strange—and stupid—that it hurt to think that, even now.

'You'd be helping me out,' Jace told her. 'Although I recognise that might not be a point in my favour.'

Eleanor flushed. 'I don't have some kind of—vendetta,'

she told him. 'Really, Jace, the past is forgotten.' It was a lie, but she said it anyway.

'Do you really think so?' Jace queried softly. 'I know I can't forget that easily.'

Eleanor's flush deepened. She didn't know what Jace was talking about, but she knew there were plenty of things she couldn't forget. Like the first time he'd kissed her, after she'd given him a chocolate cupcake she'd baked, so that she couldn't eat chocolate even now without thinking of that wonderful, breathless moment. Like how wonderful it had been to lie in his arms, the sun bathing them in gold. How he was the only person who had ever made her cry with joy.

'I don't know,' she said slowly, yet as the words came out of her mouth she realised she already knew, she'd known from the moment she'd walked in and seen Jace in her office. She might have offered a few paltry protests for form's sake, but in her heart she'd already agreed to go to Greece.

The question she had no intention of answering or even asking herself was *why*. Was it simply pressure from work— Lily would undoubtedly insist she go—or a deeper, more dangerous reason? A reason that had nothing to do with business and all to do with pleasure?

With Jace.

'Two weeks,' Jace told her, his tone turning brisk and reasonable. 'Not that long, but long enough to plan a small family party. And the weather will be fabulous. I'm sure you could use a break.'

Eleanor nodded jerkily and pulled a fresh pad of paper towards her. 'Where exactly is this party going to be?'

She saw triumph gleam in Jace's eyes, turning them silver, and his mouth curled upwards in a smile of victory. 'At my villa. I own a small island in the Cyclades.'

Her head jerked up. 'Your private *island*?'

'It's very small.'

'Sure it is,' Eleanor muttered, and uselessly scribbled 'island' on her notepad. She could hardly believe she was agreeing to this so readily, so easily, and yet she knew how little choice she really had. If Lily wanted Jace's business, and Jace wanted her to plan the party, she was left with very few choices.

But why does he want me to plan the party? And why do I want to go?

Eleanor forced the questions aside and turned to smile with sunny professionalism at Jace. 'Can you give me a few details?'

'I don't think that's necessary,' Jace replied easily. He rose from his chair, and after a second's hesitation Eleanor rose as well. 'I'm returning to Greece on Friday, and I'd like you to come with me. That should give you enough time to wrap up things here for a bit, and it will also leave enough time on the other end to plan the party.'

'Right,' she replied, her mind spinning. Friday. Greece. *Jace.*

'If you have any questions, don't hesitate to contact me,' Jace continued, matching her best, brisk and professional tone. 'Otherwise, I'll see you Friday morning. I'll send a car to pick you up at your apartment at nine o'clock?'

Eleanor nodded her acceptance, and, with an answering nod, Jace picked up his coat and was gone.

Eleanor sank back into her chair just as Lily poked her head round the door.

'Well?'

'I guess I'm going to Greece.'

'Good.' Lily nodded with smug satisfaction. 'I told him it wouldn't be a problem.' She paused, eyes narrowing. 'You did seem a little reluctant to work with Zervas before, Eleanor, which surprised me. I trust you've got over it?'

Eleanor nodded wearily, too overwhelmed to offer a defence. 'It's fine,' she said, and almost believed it.

The days between Monday and Friday flew by and crept along at the same time. Eleanor immersed herself in work, transferring clients, wrapping up details, and yet it still left her with far too much to think about.

She alternated between wondering if she was making the biggest—or perhaps the second biggest—mistake of her life, and convincing herself that this was nothing more than a business trip. It wasn't like the *biggest* mistake she'd made, which had been to fall in love with Jace Zervas in the first place.

She had no intention of doing that again.

Neither her mother nor Allie were convinced.

'I just don't see why you're going,' Allie said for the third time as they shared a Chinese takeaway in her apartment on Wednesday night. 'Or, more importantly, why he's taking you.' She lowered her chopsticks to regard Eleanor severely. 'Do you think he's interested in you again?'

'No,' Eleanor said firmly. 'It's nothing like that.'

'How can you be so sure? He kissed you, didn't he?'

'Yes, but…' She shook her head, realising she couldn't answer the question. She didn't know why Jace had kissed her. She had no idea why he wanted her to go to Greece. 'We're different people,' she stated, rather uselessly, for Allie just narrowed her eyes.

'Not that different. I just don't want this jerk to hurt you again, Eleanor. That's all.'

'He's not a jerk,' Eleanor whispered. She felt herself flush as Allie stared at her in disbelief. 'At least, not as much of one as I once thought,' she amended, and Allie snorted.

'Well, that's reassuring.'

'I suppose I'm realising that I never really knew him,' Eleanor explained slowly. 'I know we were supposedly infatuated with one another, but Jace never really talked about himself. I only realised that later—when I saw him again, and he said things…' She paused, helpless to explain. 'I never knew he had five sisters. Or he didn't get along with his father. Or—'

'Oh, help,' Allie cut her off, her eyes widening in horror. 'You're in love with him already, aren't you?'

'No!' The word was a yelp. Eleanor scrambled off the sofa and stood there, chest heaving in denial. 'No,' she said more calmly. 'Of course not. But I suppose seeing him again—for real—is important to me. Necessary. I need the closure.'

'But didn't you get that when he apologised?'

She took a breath and let it out slowly. 'Not really. I need to know that I can't fall in love with him again. That there really is nothing between us, and that we're just too different. Too changed.' She sighed, the truth coming to her as she spoke it. 'Then I'll finally be able to move on.' Why did that idea make her feel sad rather than hopeful? Was she *still* fooling herself?

'Maybe,' Allie allowed, her voice laden with doubt. 'What if you find out you can fall in love with him, Eleanor? What if you *do*?'

That was another question Eleanor couldn't answer, and didn't even dare ask.

Her mother was just as doubtful of the wisdom of Eleanor's decision, but they didn't discuss love or anything close to it. They never had.

'I wouldn't get within a hundred feet of that man,' Heather said darkly when Eleanor called her to tell her she'd be out of town, 'but if it really is just business...'

'Of course it is.' She sounded far more certain than she felt.

'I'm sure you know what you're doing,' Heather said briskly. 'And in any case, it's wonderful that Lily thinks so highly of you.'

Eleanor didn't want to argue that it was actually Jace—and his money—that Lily thought highly of. She was too tired and she had too much to do to argue the semantics. 'I'll talk to you when I get back,' she said, and after exchanging a few more pleasantries she hung up the phone.

Surveying the mess of her bedroom, the contents of her wardrobe spilled across her bed, she wondered just what to pack—and what to wear when she saw Jace tomorrow.

She settled on a pair of tailored tan trousers and a petal-pink cashmere sweater set that would have made her feel like a granny save for its hugging fit. Paired with a pair of kitten-heeled open-toed sandals, they made her feel professional and just a little bit sexy, which gave her confidence a needed boost as she waited in her building's lobby for the car Jace had sent.

The limo came promptly at nine. As the driver opened the door and Eleanor slid into the car's luxurious interior, Eleanor felt a flicker of disappointment that it was empty. Jace wasn't there.

'Mr Zervas will meet you at the airport,' the driver told her as he pulled away from the kerb. Eleanor did not reply, although she wondered what kept Jace in the city so that he couldn't share the journey to the airport with her. Not, she told herself sternly, that it mattered. Determined to focus on business—which was what this whole trip *was*—she reached for a file folder and began jotting down preliminary ideas for the party.

This activity kept her busy all the way to the airport, mainly because she wanted it to. She didn't want or need time to think, to question just why the *hell* she'd agreed to come to Greece with Jace, on the pretext of some party. She'd told her mother it was business; she'd told Allie more of the truth—that she needed closure. Yet the nerves exploding inside her, her clammy hands and growing panic all made Eleanor realise that there might be more to it than that. A lot more.

She clamped down on the train of thought before it could go anywhere, and as they arrived at the terminal she gratefully slid out of the car as the driver opened the door.

'Hello, Eleanor.'

Nearly yelping in surprise, Eleanor looked up to see Jace smiling at her. He was dressed, as she'd nearly always seen him dressed, for business, and he looked, as he always did, magnificent. Eleanor swallowed rather dryly.

'I thought you'd be late,' she said, trying not to sound flustered. 'Since you didn't come in the limo—'

'I didn't have time to drive to your apartment in Chelsea,'

Jace explained, 'so I grabbed a cab. I hope it didn't inconvenience you?'

How could a limo to her front door inconvenience her? Eleanor wondered. Or was Jace obliquely referring to the fact that she'd been disappointed? How did he *know*? 'No, of course not,' she said briskly, and Jace touched her elbow to guide her inside.

They bypassed the endless queues at the ticket counters for a discreet security checkpoint for private airline passengers.

'We're travelling on your private jet?' Eleanor practically squeaked when she realised this. 'To your private island?'

'I like my privacy.' Jace smiled, a flash of white. 'And I confess I find it more convenient. No need to book tickets or schedule flights, or be at the mercy of an airline and its asinine whims.'

The security guard waved them through, and easily, naturally, Jace put his arm around Eleanor's shoulders as he shepherded her towards the boarding area. 'Come.'

Moments later they were boarding a small, sleek, and utterly luxurious aeroplane. Eleanor took in the leather sofas and teakwood coffee tables with a sense of disbelief. She'd experienced her fair share of first class service as an event planner, yet in those cases she was arranging the luxury for her clients; *she* was the service. Here she was the one being served, and it felt amazing.

'Stretch out,' Jace said with a smile as she sat on one of the sofas. 'Enjoy yourself.'

Eleanor smiled a bit uncertainly. She was torn between enjoying herself—which this jet cried out for her to do—and keeping things businesslike. Professional. Safe.

'There will be plenty of time to plan the party later,' Jace told her with a little smile, making Eleanor wonder yet again how he knew her so well.

Because, she reminded herself as reached for the seat buckle, he didn't know her well. At all. He hadn't known her well enough ten years ago to trust her with the truth, and he certainly didn't know her now.

Moodily she stared out of the window as the plane began to taxi down the runway. Within minutes they were lifting off, leaving the dank grey March skies for the vast blue above.

One of Jace's staff came to offer drinks, and Eleanor accepted a glass of orange juice. She took a sip and set it down, too restless and uneasy to drink more. She fidgeted with the clasp on her seat belt, crossed and recrossed her legs, and stared blindly out at the endless blue sky.

'You can undo your seat belt now if you like,' Jace said, and Eleanor jerked her head around. He sat stretched out on the sofa opposite her.

'Oh, yes,' she mumbled, flicking again at the clasp. 'All right.' She undid the belt and stretched her legs out, feeling as if she were participating in a charade. She didn't feel remotely relaxed, and she doubted she was giving a good impression of it either.

'Why are you so tense, Eleanor?' Jace asked. 'You look drawn tighter than a bow.'

'I feel tense,' Eleanor admitted. 'And why shouldn't I be?' she added with a note of challenge. 'I don't even know why I'm here.'

Something dark—a shadow of pain, or perhaps even uncertainty—flickered in Jace's eyes. 'To plan my father's birthday party.'

'I know, but—' Eleanor let out a long, exasperated breath. 'I don't understand why you chose me to plan this party. It makes no sense. Someone local, with Greek contacts, would have been—'

'I didn't want someone local,' Jace cut across her quietly. 'Even if it made sense.'

His words sounded like a confession, and they created a sudden awareness in the air; it crackled like a current between them. 'Well, you should have,' Eleanor replied robustly in a desperate bid to ignore the current that practically pulled her out of her seat towards Jace.

Could she *ever* resist him?

'I didn't want someone local,' Jace repeated softly. 'I wanted you.'

Eleanor felt as if all the breath had been robbed from her body; her mind spun emptily and her chest hurt. She stared at Jace, pulled by the magnetic silver of his eyes, the faint smile curling his mouth—how she remembered that mouth, how it felt, how it tasted—

Don't. Don't remember, don't want—

Somehow she managed to draw a breath in, and the desperate dizziness receded. She reached for her orange juice and took a much-needed sip. 'Don't, Jace.'

'And,' Jace continued, leaning forward, 'you want me.'

'What?' The word was a yelp, a squeal, and it didn't hold the disdain Eleanor wanted it to, nor even the outrage. She sounded like a kicked puppy. She drew herself up, replacing her juice on the table with a decisive clink. 'Don't do this, Jace.'

'I didn't want to,' Jace replied. His voice was low even though his smile remained wry, light. 'Why do you think you didn't hear from me for three months? I've been trying to forget you, Eleanor, and the damnable truth is I can't.'

He almost sounded annoyed, and that made Eleanor smile faintly. She knew just how he felt. Then reality came crashing in. 'Is that why you hired me, Jace? To—to—have some kind of—' She sputtered uselessly, unable to say the word. *Affair.*

Meaningless. Sordid.

What else could he possibly want?

'I'm talking about more than just physical attraction,' Jace said, his voice soft and yet steely, and Eleanor stiffened.

What could he possibly mean? And why did his words terrify her so much? She couldn't untangle the sudden fierce emotion within her: surprise, alarm, fear, *hope*.

'What do you mean?' she asked. She tried to sound

dismissive but came off as demanding instead. She *wanted* to know, yet she was still afraid to hear his answer.

Jace didn't reply for a long moment. He looked pensive, guarded, as if he were hiding his heart as much as she was. 'I'm not sure.'

Eleanor sank back against the soft leather cushions. 'Okay...'

'I don't know what can be between us,' Jace continued. His tone was matter-of-fact, almost flat, yet his words raced right to Eleanor's nerve endings and made her whole self tingle with both longing and fear. 'All I know is I haven't been able to put you from my mind these last three months.' He turned back to her, his expression hard and determined. 'I said goodbye to you in New York, Eleanor, and I meant it. I wanted to walk away. God knows it's easier.'

Eleanor couldn't speak. Her throat was too tight, so she just nodded—jerkily—instead. It *was* easier. Or at least it was supposed to be.

'But it hasn't been easier,' Jace continued, his voice roughening with emotion. 'It's been hell. And so I decided to invite you to Greece—and forget the party, frankly—because I want to figure out what this is between us, and the only way I know of doing that is seeing you. Being with you. Knowing you, this new you, and you knowing me. And whatever *this* is, maybe it will go somewhere, and maybe it won't.' He let out a short, sharp laugh that ended on a ragged sigh. 'That's quite an appealing proposition, isn't it?' He shook his head and glanced away, rubbing his jaw with one hand. 'I must be crazy.'

Eleanor blinked and swallowed, trying to ease the tightness in her throat. She'd expected Jace to offer her some kind of smooth suggestion of seduction; if she was honest, yes, she'd expected it from the beginning, no matter what she'd managed to convince herself about this trip being business.

But this? This was real. Honesty. Vulnerability. It sent her spinning into a void of unknowing, uncertainty, because she couldn't scoff or sneer or pretend. Jace had been honest, and he deserved an honest answer. 'No,' she finally managed, her voice scratchy, 'you're not.' Jace turned to look at her sharply, and Eleanor smiled weakly. 'Crazy, that is.'

A corner of his mouth quirked up, although his gaze remained intently, intensely fastened on hers, filled with a wary hope she both felt and understood. 'I'm not?'

She shook her head. She didn't trust herself to say anything; she didn't even know what she would say, or what she felt. Like Jace, she knew there was still something between them. She just didn't know what it was. A remnant of their youthful infatuation? Or something new? And if it was something new, it was far too tender and fragile to test it, to trust it.

She had no idea what to do, and the thought of spending two weeks in Jace's company—with him—frightened and exhilarated her more than anything ever had before. She'd been nervous before; now she was terrified.

Thankfully Jace must have sensed this, or maybe he was feeling it himself, for he leaned forward to touch her hand— lightly, so lightly—and, smiling, said, 'It's a long flight, and you look exhausted. You should get some rest.'

Eleanor nodded, grateful for the escape sleep would provide…if only she could will it to come.

Jace watched Eleanor out of the corner of his eye as she shifted and fidgeted on the sofa, trying to get comfortable. Her eyes were closed, clenched shut really, and she didn't look remotely relaxed.

Yet why should she be? He certainly wasn't. Jace stared down at the papers he'd spread out on his table tray, notes on the latest business meeting regarding an acquisition of a plastics company in Germany. Important information, yet he couldn't process a single detail. His mind was spinning from what he'd just told Eleanor…hell, what he'd just told himself. He'd never intended to say any of that. He'd never meant even to think it.

He still didn't know what it meant, what it could mean

for the next few weeks, or even longer than that—who knew
how long? What was he thinking? Wanting? He'd known
he wanted—needed, even—to see Eleanor again, to get her
out of his system, or maybe back into it… He didn't know
which, didn't know which he even wanted. He felt as if the
course he'd set for himself, the life he'd planned on, had
been shipwrecked and he were left tossed on a sea of new
possibilities…possibilities that were bewildering and strange
and perhaps unwelcome. Perhaps exciting. He didn't know
what he wanted any more, what shape he hoped his life would
take.

Annoyed with himself, Jace let out a frustrated breath and
turned determinedly back to his papers. Enough wondering.
Enough thinking. Eleanor was here with him, and he would
be satisfied with that for now.

CHAPTER EIGHT

SHE must have dozed, for when Eleanor woke up, blinking groggily, she could tell some time had passed. How much she had no idea, but Jace was no longer sitting next to her, and her hair, when she patted it experimentally, was sticking up in several different directions.

Great. So much for her poised, polished, *professional* appearance. Yet hadn't that been a charade anyway?

I want to figure out what this is between us, and the only way I know of doing that is seeing you. Being with you.

Jace's words echoed through Eleanor's mind, still surprising her with their honesty. Her reaction, fizzing with excitement and uncertainty, surprised her too. She'd been so careful to be professional with Jace, and her ever-captive heart had betrayed her. She still wanted him. Maybe she even loved him. Yet how could you love someone you didn't even know, weren't sure you ever really knew? And if she didn't love him, then this whole thing was nothing but immature infatuation, and she needed to get it out of her system. Return to New York a freed woman. Maybe that was what Jace wanted as well. Freedom, not love.

'You're awake.'

Eleanor turned around in her seat to see Jace standing in the aisle. He'd exchanged his business suit for a casual polo shirt and khakis, and he looked wonderful. Relaxed and confident and approachable, like the old Jace. Not the harsh, hardened, businessman she'd already become accustomed to.

'Sorry to conk out like that. How long did I sleep?'

'Nearly four hours. We'll be there in another couple of hours. Do you want something to eat?'

In answer Eleanor's stomach rumbled audibly, and Jace grinned. 'I remember how loudly your stomach growls when you're hungry. I always knew it was feeding time.'

'I am hungry,' Eleanor admitted. It still made her feel uneasy—vulnerable—for Jace to recall those sweet, forbidden memories. Little things, silly things, and yet so achingly precious.

Jace raised a hand, and within seconds a staff member arrived with a tray of food. Eleanor took in the fresh fruit, the plates of salad and sandwiches, and realised she wasn't just hungry, she was starving.

'Dig in,' Jace said, and she did.

'So where exactly are we going?' Eleanor asked after she'd finished most of her sandwich and salad. She toyed with a bit of pineapple on her plate, shredding the succulent fruit with the tines of her fork.

'My island. It's near Naxos. Like I said, very small.'

Eleanor looked up, her eyes narrowing speculatively. 'How small?'

Jace waved a hand in dismissal. 'A couple of kilometers, no more.'

'And there's nothing on it but your villa?'

'A few staff houses, an airstrip.'

'Really.' She let out a reluctant laugh. 'I always knew you were rich, but I didn't know you were *Fantasy-Island*-type rich.'

Jace arched his eyebrows. 'What does that mean exactly?'

'Private jet, private island.' Eleanor shrugged. 'It's like a soap opera.'

'They are conveniences as well as luxuries. And I have worked hard to earn them, I must admit.'

'You have?' Why did this surprise her? She supposed it was because after Jace had left, she'd painted him in her mind as the spoiled son of a shipping magnate. It was easier to accept his abandonment that way. Over the years she'd embroidered that image, yet now she realised—of course—that might not be who Jace was—or ever had been—at all.

She really didn't know him.

She popped the piece of pineapple in her mouth. 'So what did you do to earn it?'

'Investments. Financial management.'

'I thought your father was in shipping.'

'He is. But I did not go into my father's business.' A new, steely note had entered Jace's voice although his posture and expression were both still easy and relaxed. 'He wanted a dynasty, and neither of us believed that to be a possibility.'

Eleanor straightened in her seat. She cleared her throat, wanting to ask the question that remained unspoken between them yet knowing there was so much more to Jace's alleged infertility than the condition itself; years of heartache and family strife seemed to accompany it. 'Did you…get tested again?' she finally asked. Jace's expression didn't change. 'For fertility?'

'Yes.' He gave a little shrug, as though the matter was of no consequence. Perhaps it wasn't. 'I have limited fertility, the doctor says.'

Eleanor's heart twisted, a little wrench she should have long become used to when the topic turned to children. 'That's pretty good, isn't it?' It was possibility, hope. More than she would ever have. Limited was better than nothing.

Jace shrugged again. 'Whether or not I can have children has not been a pressing issue for me as of late.' The news should have reassured her, especially considering her own situation, yet somehow it just made her sad. So much lost. So much gone…for both of them.

Jace gave her the ghost of a smile, no more than a shadow passing across his face. 'Apparently, after childhood mumps, limited fertility can return in later years.' He shook his head and laughed softly, although the sound held little humour. 'Amazing, a simple Internet search could have saved us both so much heartache.'

'I don't know about that,' Eleanor said, and Jace stilled, his expression becoming alert and a little wary.

'What do you mean, Eleanor?'

She shrugged. 'Even if you knew the baby was yours, Jace, would you have stayed?' The question seemed to drop into the stillness, tautening the very air between them.

Jace tensed, and Eleanor saw in the steely silver glint in his eyes, the thinning of his mouth, that he was angry. She'd made him angry with her question. 'Of course I would have. I would never walk away from my own child.'

She didn't want to have this fight. She didn't want to feel this hurt. Shrugging again, Eleanor turned to look out of the window, sunlight shimmering on the faint wisps of cloud. 'You didn't trust me enough to give me a chance to trust you,' she said quietly. 'No matter what might be between us now, Jace, there will always be that.'

'Then you can't forgive?'

'I'm not saying that. I'm just saying that we've never had a chance to trust each other.' She turned back to look at him directly, compelled to honesty even though she'd wanted to avoid this conversation. 'It's not something that ever comes easily, and it certainly won't now, with our history.' *Not,* she added silently, *when I'm scared to trust you. To love you.*

Jace was silent for a long moment, and Eleanor waited and watched. It was only when he spoke again that she realised she'd been holding her breath. 'Then I suppose we'll just have to see what happens,' he finally said, a faint smile curving his lips even though his eyes looked shadowed and sad. 'And what we allow to happen.'

They steered clear of such intense topics for the rest of the flight, chatting about the weather and films and other innocuous things, until Jace excused himself to finish his work before they landed on Naxos to transfer to a smaller plane that would take them on the short flight to his island.

Eleanor didn't bother to pretend to work; her nerves were leaping and jumping inside her too much to make sense of anything. She felt an unsettling mix of anticipation and alarm. The sun had set and the sky was a deep and endless black, the pinpoints of a million stars reflected in the sea below. As the island came into view, Eleanor saw the lights of Naxos's main village shimmer along the harbour.

The plane taxied to a stop and Eleanor reached for her things. Jace shepherded her out of the plane, and she barely had a chance to view the huddled whitewashed buildings of Naxos in the distance as she walked across the tarmac to a much smaller plane.

The flight to Jace's island took all of ten minutes, and when the plane landed there were no friendly village lights to welcome them. The island was dark, lost on a sea of night, and despite the balmy air Eleanor couldn't quite keep from shivering.

She tilted her head up to take in the endless sky, spangled with stars. 'I don't think I've ever seen so many stars.'

'I don't think you can see a single star in New York,' Jace agreed. 'Come. My staff will see to our bags.'

Eleanor followed him into an open-topped Jeep. She was conscious of so many things: the emptiness all around them of sea and sky, the deep darkness of the night, and the fact that, despite the discreet staff moving their luggage into another waiting Jeep, she felt as if they were the only two people left on earth.

Jace started the Jeep, flicking on the headlights, which barely pierced the darkness, unrelieved by the flicker of a single street lamp or house light. They were alone. On an island. In the middle of the sea.

Eleanor swallowed and glanced sideways at Jace. As she did she became conscious of yet another thing: how different he was here, in his casual clothes, navigating the rocky, rutted road that skirted the sea as it wound round an outcropping of rock. Here he wasn't the college student or the businessman; he was someone else entirely.

She wondered just who that was.

'It's after eleven o'clock at night,' Jace told her, 'but it's still early in East Coast time. Would you like something to eat?'

'Maybe,' Eleanor allowed. She felt tired and yet inexorably, impossibly alive, thrilled and alarmed and wary of all these new sights, sounds, and changes. 'Something small would be nice,' she decided, and Jace flashed her a quick smile.

'I'll have my cook prepare something. You can freshen up and change if you like. The luggage is right behind us.'

Jace drove the Jeep around another curve and the villa came into view: a huge, sprawling whitewashed structure, every window and doorframe spilling a riot of bougainvillea, lights glimmering from inside. Jace killed the engine on the Jeep and turned to Eleanor.

'Welcome.'

A smiling, red-cheeked woman with her hair caught up in a headscarf met them on the doorstep.

She spoke rapidly in Greek, and Jace nodded and smiled his approval. Then, in halting English, she spoke to Eleanor. 'Welcome, Miss Langley. We are happy to see you here.'

'Thank you,' Eleanor murmured. Jace touched her shoulder.

'This is Agathe. She takes care of just about everything for me.' He smiled again at Agathe and then Eleanor followed her upstairs.

Agathe led her to a spacious suite of rooms overlooking the gardens at the back of the villa, bathed in moonlight; Eleanor could only make out the twisted trunks of olive trees and the glint of the sea at their edge.

Her luggage arrived moments later, and she took the opportunity to change her clothes and wash her face. Even though it was now nearing midnight, she felt energised and awake and alive.

Agathe had gone to see to their dinner preparations, and, dressed in a pair of cotton capris and a loose, flowing top in pale green, Eleanor stepped out to explore the villa…and to find Jace.

The air was dry and smelled faintly of lavender and thyme; through the open windows Eleanor could hear the gentle shooshing of the waves on the sand. She walked down the tiled hallway to the front stairs, her hand skimming the wrought-iron bannister. The foyer below was empty, and once downstairs she peeked into a large, comfortable-looking living room and a dining room with a table that looked to seat at least twenty. Both were dark and empty.

She wandered towards the back of the house, drawn by the light spilling from an open doorway and the tempting aroma of lemon and garlic.

She stepped into the kitchen to see Agathe busy at the stove, and, to her surprise, Jace setting the table in the alcove that overlooked the water. He'd changed as well, and showered if the damp hair curling at his nape were anything to go by. Eleanor swallowed. He looked wonderful.

Jace glanced up as she stood in the doorway, and smiled easily. 'Come in! Agathe has made a feast, as always.'

Agathe protested even as she placed dish upon dish on the table. Eleanor took in the Greek salad bursting with plump tomatoes and cucumber, a thick wedge of feta cheese resting on top, and the freshly grilled souvlaki, still on its skewer. There was a lentil soup garnished with olives and crusty bread, and several traditional Greek dips to accompany it.

'I can never eat all this,' Eleanor produced, laughing a little.

'You must try,' Jace replied as he pulled out her chair. 'After all, food is love.'

Love. Eleanor swallowed again. That was a word they'd never talked about, not ten years ago and certainly not now. Oh, she'd thought it plenty of times; she'd certainly believed it before Jace had walked away. Yet now just the idea of love—the mere mention of it—made her palms slick and nerves flutter from her belly to her throat.

'Thank you for this, Agathe.'

Agathe made more protesting noises before discreetly disappearing into another room. A candle flickered on the table between them, and the room was silent save for the sound of the sea coming from the open window.

'This is lovely,' Eleanor said. 'Thank you.'

Jace gave a little shrug. 'I'm afraid I'm spoiled by Agathe. She was my childhood nurse growing up, and I employed her here when she had no more charges at my family home.'

'She loves you very much.' The words popped out inadvertently, even though Eleanor didn't want to mention that dreaded L-word. Jace just smiled and spooned some tzatziki onto her plate.

'She is a good woman.'

Eleanor took a spoonful of the hearty bean soup; it was delicious. 'So do you live here most of the year?'

'When I can. I have a flat in Athens for business, but this is really my home. Or at least my escape. I've had to travel so much for work, I don't know if I could call any place my home.'

'Those corporate takeovers,' Eleanor murmured. She took another sip of soup. 'What's the real story behind you taking over Atrikides Holdings?'

Jace looked up, surprised. 'The real story?'

'I don't think it was the heartless takeover you made it out to be.'

'I try not to have any takeover be heartless.'

Eleanor raised her eyebrows. 'I had no idea you were so sensitive.'

Jace only looked amused. 'Sensitive? No. It's simply good business. Unhappy workers are never very productive.' He gave her the glimmer of a smile. 'I don't like to lose money.'

'Ah.' She reached for a piece of bread. 'And Atrikides?'

Jace shrugged. 'It was a favour to Leandro. His son was embezzling from him and he didn't have the strength to deal with it himself. He's an old man, and he doesn't have much longer to live.'

'So it was a mercy mission.'

Jace just shrugged again, and Eleanor glanced down at her plate. 'There's so much I don't know about you.'

A tiny, telling hesitation. 'Then ask.'

She didn't know what questions to ask. Where to begin. She didn't even know enough for that. 'Were you always interested in finance?' she finally asked. 'Starting your own company?'

'Yes,' Jace answered, then added, 'but it became more important to me.'

'When?'

He paused. 'Ten years ago.'

Eleanor nodded slowly in acceptance. Ten years ago. Of course. The same time her work had become more important to her; it had filled the empty spaces in her heart, her womb. Jace, in his own way, had suffered a similar loss.

'Well,' Jace said when she didn't reply, 'if you won't ask questions, I will. What made you decide to become an event planner?'

'I needed to do something, and my mother suggested the internship. Premier Planning was her company before she retired.'

'So you're the boss's daughter?'

Eleanor shrugged. 'She certainly didn't give me any hand-outs. I had to apply for the internship like anyone else, and work my way up.'

'And what about your degree in restaurant management?'

Eleanor gave him a small smile even though his question—his ignorance—hurt. 'I never finished my degree.'

'You didn't? Why not?'

She shook her head, exasperated now. Jet lag must have caught up with her, for she suddenly felt unbearably weary. 'I was pregnant, and I intended to keep the baby. I dropped out.'

Jace looked startled, a streak of something like pain flashing in his eyes, and Eleanor knew he was realising how much he didn't know. Didn't understand. Just as she felt with him. They really did need to begin all over again—if they could.

'But after?' he persisted after a moment. 'Couldn't you have gone back?'

'I didn't want to,' Eleanor said flatly. 'Everything had changed.' She didn't want to talk about it with Jace, even though at least part of her acknowledged they would have to talk about it some time…if they wanted to have any hope of—anything—in the future. 'My turn for questions,' she said. 'What's your favourite colour?'

Jace looked startled again, but then his face relaxed in an easy smile and Eleanor knew he was as glad as she was for a safer topic of conversation. 'Purple.'

'No way.'

He arched an eyebrow. 'What? Not manly enough?'

Eleanor let out a reluctant laugh. 'There's no way purple is your favourite colour. I may not know you that well, but I know that.'

He sighed in mock defeat. 'All right, you win. It's blue.'

'Light blue or dark blue?'

'Dark. And you?'

'Orange.'

'Really?'

Eleanor smiled. 'Yes, but I picked it as my favourite colour in first grade because no one else liked it. I guess I wanted to be different.'

'You always were stubborn.'

'Determined, I call it.' Sometimes it had been the only thing that had kept her going. Another wave of fatigue crashed over her and she pushed her plate away. 'This was delicious, but I think the flight is finally catching up with me. I'm about to fall asleep in my chair.'

'Then we'd better get you to bed.'

His words, given with such lazy amusement, made aware-ness race through Eleanor's veins so she suddenly felt rather unbearably awake. She stood up awkwardly. 'Thank you for the meal—'

'Let me show you to your room.'

'I remember—'

'I'm a gentleman.'

Wordlessly Eleanor let him lead her from the kitchen. Her heart had begun thudding hard against her chest, and she wondered what might happen. What she wanted to happen.

Upstairs the hallway was dark, lit only by a wash of moonlight from the windows at its end. Jace led her to her door and she placed her hand on its knob, turning around so her back was pressed against the wood. 'Thank you...' The word ended in a whisper of breath for Jace was close. Very close. And she had a feeling he was going to kiss her.

She wanted him to kiss her.

He smiled at her and brushed a strand of hair away from her face, tucking it behind her ear so his thumb skimmed her cheek. Eleanor closed her eyes. The moment before his lips brushed hers seemed endless, agonising, because she wasn't sure he was even going to do it and she didn't want to open her eyes to find out.

Finally, *finally* his lips touched hers in a feather-light kiss that seemed to be more of a promise than a possession, because before Eleanor could part her lips or respond in any way—it was so sweet—he had stepped away.

Her eyes flew open and she stared at him. He gazed back at her with a rueful, almost sad smile. 'Goodnight, Eleanor.'

Before she could respond—or even think—he was already disappearing down the hallway, lost in the shadows.

Jace strode out of the villa, frustration and fury and even fear all warring within him. What had he done? And why had he done it?

He made his way down the track to the beach, awash in silver in the moonlight. A few metres away the waves crashed blackly onto the shore. Jace yanked his shirt over his head and kicked his trousers off and then, with one deep breath, he dived into the surf.

The water was cold—it was still early spring—and it made his head ache as he swam through the waves, breaking to the surface only when his lungs hurt and his head pounded.

He treaded water as he gazed up at the ink-black sky scattered with stars and wondered just why he'd brought Eleanor to Greece.

It had seemed like such a good idea when he'd spoken to Alecia. It had made sense when he'd flown to New York on the pretence of needing to visit Atrikides Holdings, which was managing just fine under Leandro's nephew. He'd justified it to himself because he'd needed to see her, because his body was hungry and his soul restless knowing she was there, knowing she'd never lied to him, thinking that maybe there could have been something between them all these years. Maybe there still could be.

Yet what he hadn't counted on was how risky it was. Eleanor wasn't interested in an emotionless affair. He'd *known* that, and yet he'd still brought her here as if they could have something else. Something more. As if he wanted that, which, God help him, maybe he did.

Even though he'd determined for ten years—and longer than that, *for ever*—never to lose his heart to anyone. Never to even have a heart to lose.

Jace cursed out loud, to the sky, the words lost in the rush of the waves. His body ached with fatigue and cold and, after another second of useless treading water—going nowhere— he headed back towards the shore.

Everything had changed when he'd kissed Eleanor—such a nothing little kiss, barely a brush of their lips. Yet in that fragile moment he'd realised just what he'd done by bringing Eleanor here. Not only had he opened himself up to possible pain and loss, but he'd exposed Eleanor to it as well. He could hurt her. Again.

Back on the beach Jace towelled himself off with his shirt and then sat on the cold, hard sand to dry off. He wasn't ready to go back into the villa, to a lonely bed just two doors from where Eleanor slept. Or maybe she wasn't sleeping. Maybe she was tossing restlessly just as he surely would, letting the memories wash over her like the surf over the sand.

The first time they'd kissed. He'd been determined to kiss her, and she'd been skittish and nervous, flitting around her apartment, plying him with cupcakes. He'd eaten them, laughing as he did so, because they'd both known what was better than any dessert. That first kiss had been so, so sweet; it had been innocence and longing entangled together.

The first time they'd made love, one Saturday afternoon, the room mellow with sunlight. He'd traced circles on her skin with his fingers and lips and she'd laughed and told him she was ticklish.

Ticklish! He'd been a little offended, because he'd been so breathless and aching with desire, and he'd set upon a course of making her want him as much as he wanted her.

He'd succeeded admirably.

But it hadn't been just sex. She'd opened up such a life to him, a sweet, simple life, and he'd let himself fall, had willingly entered into the dream she shared of a bakery and bookshop, let it all wash over him and pull him into a fantasy world that he'd never thought to inhabit because it was all so far from his life, from his father. With Eleanor he hadn't been a useless failure. He hadn't had his shortcomings tossed back at him again and again.

With Eleanor he'd just been himself. And yet he'd still run. Jace shook his head, the memories both hurting and humiliating him.

Even if you knew the baby was yours, Jace, would you have stayed?

The question, and the fact that Eleanor could ask it, damned him. And even now Jace was shamed by her lack of trust in him. Yet why should she trust him? He hadn't proved himself or his trustworthiness in any way. He'd only failed.

And he was afraid of failing again—failing Eleanor,

failing himself—by opening this Pandora's box of possibility between them.

Staying away would have been easier. Safer. He just wished he'd had the strength to do it.

Suppressing a shiver as a chilly wind blew off the water, Jace slung his damp shirt around his neck and headed back to the villa, now no more than a darkened hulk under the sky. Inside all was quiet, the only sound the whisper of the waves. Jace peeled off his damp clothes and fell into bed naked, clenching his eyes shut as if he could keep the doubts from assailing him, the memories from claiming him.

Yet as he finally drifted off to sleep he could see Eleanor as she once was, relaxed and laughing as she held out a chocolate cupcake, and he heard her laughter as she tempted him to taste it.

He woke up craving chocolate. Craving Eleanor.

CHAPTER NINE

ELEANOR woke up to the distant, mournful clanging of bells. She scrambled from her bed and peeked out the window; the sun was already high in the sky, glinting off the water, and on a rocky hill in the distance she saw the source of the sound: goats. The bells around their necks clanged and clanked as a boy shepherded them out of sight.

She quickly showered and dressed, slipping into a pair of tailored black trousers and a crisp white button-down shirt. Work clothes. Armour. After Jace's barely there kiss last night, she needed it. She felt entirely too fragile, too fearful.

Further armed with a pad of paper and the notes she'd taken earlier, she came downstairs to the kitchen, where Agathe was setting out breakfast.

'Dinner last night was delicious,' Eleanor said, wishing she spoke Greek. Agathe smiled widely, clearly understanding enough.

She waved towards the table. 'Eat. Eat.'

Eleanor sat down and, still smiling, Agathe poured her a cup of thick Greek coffee. Eleanor helped herself to yogurt, honey, and fresh slices of melon. 'Do you know where Jace is?' she asked hesitantly, and Agathe shrugged, spreading her hands. It took her a moment to finally find the word, but when she did, it caused double shafts of disappointment and relief to slice through Eleanor.

'Work. He work.'

'Ah. Right.' Nodding her thanks, Eleanor took a sip of the coffee. That was good, she decided. Jace was working, and so would she. That was why they were here, after all. To work.

Except yesterday, on the plane, Jace had told her to forget the party. The real reason she was here was because he wanted her to be. And *she* wanted to be, which was why she had agreed in the first place. God only knew what could happen, what they would allow to happen, as Jace had said yesterday.

Moodily Eleanor speared a slice of melon. If she were a less cautious person, she'd seize this opportunity with both hands and a lot more besides. She'd let herself enjoy Greece—enjoy *Jace*—and just see what happened. Such an easy thing to do. Just *see*.

Yet she wasn't that kind of person, although perhaps she once had been. Now she was careful and cautious and kept everything close, especially her emotions. Most definitely her heart. There was nothing easy about *just seeing* at all. It was impossibly difficult, incredibly dangerous, and she wasn't sure she could do it at all. She wasn't even sure she wanted to, despite the nameless longing that swelled up inside her, spilling out.

After breakfast, since Jace had not put in an appearance, Eleanor decided to explore the villa. She'd get a sense of what would work for the party, and present Jace with some kind of initial plan. She'd need to ask him about services too; Agathe certainly couldn't do all the cooking, and supplies would have to be either flown or ferried in.

Hugging her clipboard to her chest, Eleanor strolled through the villa's front rooms that she'd glimpsed last night. Both were spacious and comfortable, the scattered sofas and rugs giving a sense of casual elegance. They'd certainly suit for a party, but as she left them for the wraparound terrace, she decided the party should be held outside.

The air was dry and fragrant, the sun warm on her face,

the sea shimmering with its light. Terracotta pots of trailing bougainvillea and herbs lined the terrace and in the distance Eleanor could still hear the goats' bells clanging. She stood for a moment on the terrace, lifting her face to the sun, and let herself simply enjoy the day.

'There you are.'

Slowly Eleanor opened her eyes. She turned around to see Jace standing in the double doors that led to the kitchen.

'Do you have *goats* on this island?'

Surprised, he raised his eyebrows. 'As a matter of fact I do.'

'Why?'

'You don't like goats?'

Eleanor suppressed a smile. 'I don't really have an opinion of them, actually.'

'Well, I find them very calming,' Jace replied, straight-faced, 'as well as incredibly cute.'

She'd forgotten what a silly sense of humour he had, how much he'd made her laugh, helplessly, holding her sides. How *happy* he'd made her feel. Now a reluctant bubble burst through her lips and she shook her head, smiling.

'Seriously.'

'We have to be serious?' Jace's face fell comically. 'Very well. When I bought this island, it was inhabited by a single farmer. He'd lived here all his life, was ferrying his poor goats and their milk and cheese to Naxos. I let him stay and he supplies the villa more than adequately.'

'And when you aren't here?'

'He uses my motorboat. He had a leaky rowboat that looked likely to capsize in a breath of wind, and he'd put a goat in it. The poor animal was terrified.'

Eleanor shook her head, not sure if she should believe him. He looked utterly sincere, yet she saw laughter lurking in his eyes, glinting in their depths, and it made her smile again, from the heart. 'Why would he take his goat to Naxos? I thought you said he sold the milk and cheese.'

'The creature was sick.' Jace took her arm, his fingers warm on her skin. 'Terribly so. Really quite nasty. You don't want to get too close to a sick goat. They're bad-tempered creatures as it is. Now come. I have a surprise for you.'

As Jace led her from the terrace all thoughts of goats, sick or otherwise, fled from her mind. She struggled to keep her tone businesslike and brisk. 'Actually I wanted to talk about the party—'

Jace waved a hand in airy dismissal. 'Plenty of time for that. Now come into the kitchen—'

'Is Agathe—?'

'She went to Naxos right after breakfast for supplies.'

'Then what—?' Eleanor stopped in the doorway of the kitchen and stared at the pile of supplies laid out on the granite worktop. Muffin pans and parchment paper, cake tins and cookie cutters. Sacks of flour, sugar, at least three dozen eggs.

Everything needed for baking. A bakery.

Eleanor swallowed. 'You got this all for me?'

'I thought you'd have some time to do what you always wanted to do,' Jace said.

'Thank you,' she said after a moment. 'It's very thoughtful.'

'There are recipe books,' Jace continued, 'although I know you liked to make your own. I remember that coffee-bean cupcake—'

Eleanor smiled wryly. That, actually, had been one of her less successful attempts. She left Jace's side to move to the worktop, letting her fingers run over the gleaming, pristine surface of a never-used cast-iron pan.

'I got everything I thought you'd need.'

'Very thorough.' He must have spent several hundred dollars, Eleanor thought. Pennies to a millionaire like him, and yet…

'So I'll leave you to it, then?' Jace asked, clearly not expecting an answer. 'Enjoy yourself, Eleanor. Go to town.'

Town, Eleanor wondered ruefully as Jace left the kitchen. Where was that? And was she supposed to enjoy herself baking? She hadn't baked so much as a single cookie in ten years.

And that had been a *decision*. One she'd made with purposeful determination.

Sighing, she pulled a cookbook towards her and flipped through its glossy pages. It reminded her of the little leather notebook she'd kept to write her own creative concoctions in. It had been well loved, covered in splotches of batter and dollops of dough, filled with excited scribbles and dreams. She didn't even know where it was now.

As she perused the tantalising items detailed in the cookbook, each with its own coloured photo, she realised none of them appealed. Baking no longer appealed. The dream of opening her own bakery had died long ago, and she had no desire to resurrect it now. She had no desire to be the woman she once was: carefree, naive, *stupid*.

Eleanor pushed the cookbook away, and then, finding herself annoyed, angry and unable to articulate why, she left the kitchen with all of its ingredients and utensils and walked back outside.

The terrace was deserted and she took the stairs down to the path that led to the beach. She kicked off her sandals—the sexy little kitten heels were ridiculous beachwear—and walked towards the water. The sand was silky-soft under her feet, the salty breeze blowing her hair into tangles as she let the waves lap her feet, the water as warm and salty as tears.

She wasn't sure how long she stood there, her hair blowing around her face, the bottoms of her dryclean-only trousers getting wet and ruined, but she knew the exact moment that Jace came onto the beach.

She didn't have to turn to know he was there, to *feel* him. She also felt his confusion, his uncertainty, perhaps even his sorrow. Sighing, she sat down hard on the sand and drew her knees up to her chest.

'Eleanor?' Jace came closer, standing a few feet away. Eleanor could see his bare, sandy feet in her peripheral vision; he'd rolled his trousers up so his ankles were bare as well. 'Is everything—?'

'I didn't feel like baking,' she said rather flatly. 'To tell you the truth, I haven't felt like baking in—in a long time.'

Jace was silent. He sat down next to her, resting his forearms on his knees. 'For about ten years?' he guessed quietly and Eleanor let out a little laugh that sounded far too bitter.

'I told you I was a different person.'

Jace nodded slowly. 'Why did you stop baking?'

'I'm not sure,' Eleanor answered. She gazed out at the waves, glittering in the sunlight. 'I haven't really stopped to analyse it, but I suppose I wanted to separate myself from the person I was because—' she let out her breath slowly '—that person didn't work.'

Next to her she felt Jace stiffen. 'What do you mean?'

Eleanor shrugged. Every conversation kept leading to this, to what had happened between them, and all the things Jace still didn't know. She wasn't ready to talk about it. She didn't want to tell Jace just how desperate, how destroyed she'd truly been after his departure. She didn't want to feel so vulnerable. Couldn't.

'After—everything,' she began hesitantly, choosing her words with care, 'I decided to change myself. Be—someone new. It just felt like something I needed to do. And like I said, I didn't feel like baking.' Baking had reminded her of Jace. Even chocolate, supposedly a woman's dearest comfort, had reminded her of Jace. She didn't eat it even now. She turned to face him. 'I know you meant well, Jace, but—but doesn't this just show how different we are? How little we know each other any more, if we ever did?' Her voice had turned ragged, edged with desperation, and she realised she didn't know what she wanted him to say. Agree or disagree? Either would bring both disappointment and relief. Both had the capacity for heartache.

'Only if baking defined you,' Jace said slowly. 'Was it who you were, or simply something you enjoyed doing?'

Eleanor scooped up a handful of sand and let it trickle through her fingers. 'Both, in a way. And neither. I think the bakery idea was a reaction to the way I grew up. I wanted to create a place that was like home, or at least the home I'd always wanted.' She gave a little laugh. 'I think I was trying to be like the mother I'd always wanted, but I'm not sure that's really who I ever was.' She turned to look at him. 'You said I've become the person I never wanted to be, Jace, and perhaps that's true. But maybe that's the person I really *am*.'

She didn't add what she was really thinking: that that was a person Jace could never want or love. She understood why she was angry now, why she was afraid. Jace might have loved the woman she once was, but he didn't love her now. Everything he'd done was to try to turn her back into that young woman—girl—and Eleanor knew she could never be her again. She didn't even want to.

'I think you're overestimating how much you've changed,' Jace said carefully. Eleanor shook her head.

'Don't, Jace—'

'I'm not talking about opening a bakery or having a high-flying career,' Jace cut her off. 'Your job isn't who you are. I'm talking about something deeper. And I think I've come to know you enough to see that hasn't changed—not as much as you think. I don't want to change you, Eleanor. I want to know you.' Jace stood up before she could reply—she didn't even know what she would say—and held out his hand. 'Come on. I can see I made a mistake buying you all those ridiculous pans. Let's do something different.'

'Okay,' Eleanor said after a moment, and, accepting his hand, she came to her feet. She glanced down at her damp, sandy trousers with a grimace. 'Whatever it is, I should probably change—'

'Definitely.' Jace scooped up one of her sandals and dangled it by a finger. 'These may do in New York, or maybe even Mykonos, but not where we're going.'

To her surprise, Eleanor felt she was smiling. She'd been dreading that conversation, yet it hadn't been as hard as she'd thought. She knew there was still more to say, but now was not the time, and she felt relieved. 'Where are we going?'

'Hiking.' Jace pulled on her hand, a smile tugging the corner of his mouth. 'It's an adventure. You must have something suitable.'

'Maybe,' Eleanor allowed, and followed him back into the house.

Ten minutes later she'd exchanged her uniform—her armour—for more casual jeans, sneakers—she had no boots—and a plain tee shirt she'd intended only to wear to bed. She hadn't dressed like this in years; in New York she'd always had to look tailored and turned out, even when off duty. Her image was part of her profession.

Now she felt both a little self-conscious and refreshingly relaxed, the sun warm on her face, her hair curling in the heat. She had not blow-dried it that morning into her usual sleek, glossy bob.

'So where are we going?' she asked Jace as he struck out down the dirt track that led in the opposite direction they'd come the night before. 'Where *is* there to go on this island?'

'I thought I'd show you the sights,' Jace replied easily. 'As few of them as they are.'

They walked in companionable silence for a quarter of an hour, the only sound the rustle of wind in the olive trees that lined the track and the shoosh of the surf on the rocks below them. Then they rounded a curve and came face to face with a goat.

Eleanor skidded to a halt, an uneasy alarm creeping over her that was a step or two down from pure panic. Jace, who had kept walking, stopped when he realised she hadn't kept up. He glanced behind him, his eyebrows arching as he saw her frozen stance.

'Eleanor…you're not scared of a *goat*?'

'Not scared precisely,' she corrected him stiffly. 'I'm a city kid, Jace. Most animals I see are safely behind cages.'

'These goats are harmless,' Jace assured her. 'I promise.' As if to contradict him, the goat bleated loudly. Eleanor jumped. She'd never thought a bleat could sound so menacing. 'Just walk past her,' Jace assured her. 'She won't even care.'

'How do you know it's a she?'

'Her name is on the bell.' He pointed to the tarnished bell hanging around the goat's scruffy neck. 'See? Tisiphone.'

'Tisiphone? Isn't that one of the Furies?'

'Spiro likes Greek mythology,' Jace said quickly. He sounded earnest, but Eleanor could see he was trying not to smile. 'Honestly, it's no more than that.'

'And not the fact that these goats might be bad-tempered?' Eleanor countered. 'Like you told me this morning?'

'Only when on boats.'

Eleanor laughed, the sound rising from within her, freeing her somehow, loosening all those tightly held parts of herself. She wasn't *really* afraid. Well, maybe only a little. But with Jace standing just a few feet away, smiling, relaxed, his eyes warm and steady on her, she felt as if she could do anything. She could certainly walk past a goat.

Taking a deep breath, Eleanor marched rather quickly past the animal, her head held high. She let out her breath in a long shaky shudder as Jace put his arm around her shoulder.

'See? Not so bad.'

'Not so cute, either,' she muttered, and he gave out a shout of laughter, pulling her close to his side.

The contact, the intimacy, both physical and emotional, stole the breath from her lungs. She had missed this so much. This closeness, this connection. This was what being known was all about: letting another person see all the silly and stupid and sick parts of yourself, as well as all the wonderful and beautiful things. All of it, everything, out there, exposed, accepted. She craved it, and yet still it scared her.

'We need to climb now,' Jace told her, sparing her sneakers a single, dubious glance before he led her off the dirt road and straight into the scrubby hills dotted with lavender bushes and the twisted, gnarled trunks of olive trees. 'Careful. You can sprain your ankle on one of these loose rocks.'

Nodding, Eleanor picked her way carefully across the tumbled boulders. She stumbled once, and Jace was there in an instant, his hand holding hers with firm tenderness. Even when she'd righted herself he didn't let go.

They walked through the hills for another quarter of an hour before Jace stopped in what appeared to be nothing more than a rock-strewn meadow and nodded in approval. 'Here we are.'

'What—?'

'Look,' he said softly. 'Do you see?'

Eleanor looked around, taking in the scrubby bushes and twisted trees, the rocks lying in neat rows…and then she saw. Out of the wilderness there was order, the crumbling foundations of a house—many houses—hidden among the scrub.

'It was a village,' Jace said quietly. 'Two thousand years ago.' He walked over to a low wall and touched one of the ancient stones. 'I've done a little amateur archaeology, and found a few bits. Clay pots, a broken pipe. Fascinating stuff.'

Eleanor walked between two rows of walls, realising after a moment she was actually walking down a street. It was beautiful, eerie, and a little sad. 'What happened?' she asked as she stepped in the gap between two walls: a doorway. 'Why did it all fall to ruin?'

Jace shrugged. 'A flood, a famine, plague or pirates? Who knows? Something happened that forced them to flee—but I did a little research to find out where they all went.'

Eleanor turned around. 'They went somewhere?'

He nodded, smiling. 'Yes, there's an archaeological dig on Naxos that shows some of the same pieces of pottery and sculpture that were here. Historians think it's likely that they took a boat over there and started again.'

'Just like the goat.'

'Exactly.'

They lapsed into silence and Eleanor gazed at all the ruined houses, now no more than lines of stone in the dirt. She could make out an entire village now, a whole society, and she felt a strange pang of sorrow. 'And they never came back?' she asked, hearing a wistful note in her voice.

Jace glanced around at the ruins, bemused. 'So it would appear.'

'I suppose they learned you can never go back,' Eleanor said. Her words sounded heavy, too heavy, and she wondered what she was really talking about.

Jace glanced at her sharply, clearly aware of the double entendre. 'No, you can't,' he agreed. 'But you can always go forward. Like they did.' He reached for her hand, lacing his fingers through hers. Eleanor let him, let him lead her back down the hillside. 'And forward is better,' he continued lightly. 'You should see the ruins at Naxos. Now those are amazing.'

Eleanor laughed, glad the moment had been defused. She didn't want to feel sad or worried or afraid. She just wanted to enjoy being with Jace.

And she *was*. That was the wonderful thing, she thought as they walked back down the dusty road. Somehow Jace had managed to dispel her fears and her worries, and she felt carefree and relaxed as she let the wind blow her tangled hair away from her face, her hand still held in Jace's.

By the time they reached the villa, Eleanor was hot and sweaty, and when Jace suggested a swim she accepted with alacrity.

Yet as she slipped into the relatively modest one-piece she'd brought she found herself conscious of all the bare skin she was showing…all the bare skin *Jace* would be showing, and her temperature soared higher.

He was already at the beach when she arrived, a towel

wrapped firmly around her waist. Eleanor couldn't tear her gaze away from him; his chest gleamed bronze and he walked with a loose-limbed elegance, every muscle rippling with easy power. He looked wonderful, amazing, and her body kicked into gear, her heart thudding and a lazy warmth spiralling upwards inside her. He turned and smiled at her, his warm gaze sweeping over her with obvious appreciation. Eleanor's whole body tingled.

Jace stretched out his hand. 'Come on in. The water's fine this time of year.'

Despite the warmth of the sun, Eleanor thought the churning waves looked decidedly chilly. 'It's quite early to swim, isn't it?' she asked, chewing her lower lip. 'It's still only March.'

'End of March,' Jace replied and dived neatly into the water.

Emboldened, Eleanor followed suit. Seconds later she felt as if her entire body had been encased in ice. 'Aargh!' She came up gasping and choking on a mouthful of salt water. Finding her footing on the sandy bottom, she glared at Jace. 'It's freezing!'

'Bracing, we call it,' Jace replied with a grin. 'And didn't you grow up spending your summers on Long Island? You should be used to this!'

'We never swam in March,' Eleanor grumbled, but she was laughing inside, and she couldn't contain her grin as she struck out through the water to be near Jace.

They swam for nearly an hour, laughing and playing in the water, until Jace informed Eleanor that her lips were blue. Before she could form a protest, he'd scooped her up in his arms, holding her against his chest as he strode from the sea. Eleanor's laughter died in her throat as she pressed her cheek against Jace's bare, dripping chest—she just couldn't help herself—and let him take her into the villa.

He carried her all the way upstairs, to her bedroom door, and there he set her down, her body sliding sinuously against his before he steadied her on her feet. Their faces were inches apart and Eleanor didn't speak, couldn't speak. All she could do was wait, breathless, for Jace to kiss her.

He didn't. Smiling, he touched her cheek with his cold fingers and said, 'I'll see you at dinner. Seven o'clock. And don't wear another black business suit. I want it to be special.' Pressing one finger against her lips—which parted instinctively—he left.

Shivering, aching with desire, Eleanor sagged against her door. What did Jace mean by special? And why hadn't he kissed her again? It must have been glaringly obvious that she wanted him to, that she'd been waiting for him to.

Sighing, Eleanor turned inside to her bedroom. Dinner seemed ages away.

Jace strode from the villa, whistling. He felt good, relaxed, *happy*. It made him aware of how long it had been since he'd felt that way, how Eleanor made him feel that way. He'd come to Boston all those years ago looking for a new beginning, a new life away from his father and his disappointment. He'd thought he'd found it with Eleanor. And maybe he hadn't then—but maybe he could now.

This afternoon had surprised him with its simple pleasures. He'd loved being with Eleanor, loved seeing her relaxed and happy as he had been. And, he realised, he'd loved being with *this* Eleanor, the one who had grown and changed yet still had glimmers of the woman she'd once been, the one he'd known. The youthful naiveté might be gone, but it had been replaced with something better and deeper: strength, as well as courage. He admired Eleanor for both what she'd endured and achieved. And more than admired, Jace acknowledged, which made him think of a dusty trophy or distant celebrity

Yet what did he feel for Eleanor? What was he doing here? What were *they* doing?

The tuneless whistle died on his lips as he considered the question. He'd loved spending time with Eleanor, but did he love her? Was he taking her heart in his hands, only to be poised to break it?

To hurt her—destroy her, even? Again.

Or as he'd said before, could they go forward, which was so much better than going back, and build something new? Something amazing?

Jace closed his eyes. He hated that he was afraid. He wanted her so much—he'd nearly accepted her silent invitation back at her bedroom door—but he didn't want to hurt her. Yet hurt and love came hand in hand, because when someone trusted you—cared for you—you were bound, at some point, to let them down.

Or was *he* the one afraid of getting hurt?

Jace opened his eyes. He knew there were no answers. He wouldn't let his own questions—his own doubts—stop him from what was surely the sweetest time of his life. These days with Eleanor were precious, and he wouldn't waste them. He would treasure and savour them.

He hadn't kissed Eleanor this afternoon because he'd wanted to wait, he wanted to be sure she was ready in both her heart and her body.

As his own body made the insistent ache of its unsatisfied desire known Jace hoped Eleanor would be ready tonight.

He certainly was.

The sun was just starting to sink below the sea, causing its placid surface to shimmer with golden light, as Eleanor slipped on the cocktail dress she'd brought. She glanced at her reflection, lips pursed as she wondered if she was trying too hard.

The dress was sexy, probably the sexiest thing she owned. The stretchy material crossed in front, the plunging neckline accentuating the curve of her breasts. She wore a sparkly snowflake pendant she'd found at a market stall in Greenwich Village, and it nestled snugly between her breasts. The dress's skirt ended above her knees and swirled out as she walked, the silky material caressing her bare legs. She left her hair loose and her face free of make-up; the dress, she decided, was enough.

Slipping on a pair of high-heeled black sandals, she headed downstairs to meet Jace. From the top of the stairway she saw a spill of light coming from the living room, and her heart began to beat so fiercely she was sure Jace would be able to see it through the thin fabric of her dress.

Taking a deep breath, she entered the room. Jace turned as soon as he heard her, a smile lightening and softening his features. He wore a crisp white shirt and a pair of dark trousers, both exquisitely tailored and speaking of casual elegance. His admiring gaze swept her from head to toe, a grin tugging at the corner of his mouth.

'I thought I said no black.'

Eleanor pretended to pout. 'This is hardly a business suit.'

'No, indeed it is not.' Wicked humour glinted in his eyes and Eleanor's heart picked up its pace so it felt as if it were struggling right out of her throat. She felt so nervous, and yet so alive, so happy. It was scary, feeling this much. Feeling this happy.

'I thought we'd eat on the terrace. It's a warm night.'

'Sounds good.'

'May I get you a drink beforehand?' Jace gestured to the array of drinks displayed on an antique table.

'Um, no. Just wine with dinner.' She smiled, resisting the urge to wipe her palms down the sides of her dress. Her voice sounded strained, shaky, and, seeing that Jace noticed, she let out a little laugh. 'It's strange, but I feel nervous.'

He arched an eyebrow. 'Why?'

'I don't know,' Eleanor admitted. 'I suppose…because… this all feels so new. Like we're starting over.'

'We are.' His smile warmed her straight through, and she felt her body tingle with awareness and longing and something deeper…hope. Faith. Maybe it would be all right. Maybe this could work. Maybe they *could* start over. She smiled back.

Jace reached for her hand. 'Come. Let's go out to the terrace.'

She let him lead her just as she had that afternoon. Hazily Eleanor thought she'd probably like Jace to hold her hand for ever. She loved how easily his fingers laced through hers, how protected and cherished she felt from such a small and simple gesture.

Outside a candlelit table had been elegantly laid for two; Agathe was nowhere in sight. Jace pulled out her chair and laid the heavy damask napkin in her lap, then poured her a glass of wine, the rich red liquid glinting in the candlelight. After filling his own glass, he raised it, and Eleanor did likewise. '*Opa*,' he said, and Eleanor murmured it back before they both drank.

'So what does *opa* mean?' she asked once she'd set her wine glass back down.

'I don't know if there is a direct translation, but something close to cheers or—what is it you say in English?' He pursed his lips. 'Hooray.' Jace grinned. 'But if we were going to be truly traditional, we'd throw our plates on the ground.'

Eleanor widened her eyes in mock horror. 'And waste good food?' She speared a plump olive resting on top of her Greek salad. 'I don't think so.'

'My sentiments exactly.'

The meal passed quickly as Agathe slipped in and out with dish after delectable dish, and Jace kept her wine glass amply filled. Eleanor's nerves seemed to have evaporated in the warmth of his smile, the heat of his gaze. By dessert, rich, honey-soaked baklava, Eleanor felt entirely at ease and utterly relaxed.

She propped her chin on her hands and gazed at Jace speculatively, enjoying the way the candlelight glinted on his hair and caught the silvery depths of his eyes. He lounged back in his chair, a smile curving the mouth Eleanor had spent a good part of the evening gazing at, remembering how it felt on hers.

'What are you thinking?' Jace asked, and Eleanor gave a little shrug.

'Lots of things.'

'Such as?'

She wasn't quite relaxed enough to admit the true direction of her thoughts. 'That I like olives. I never did as a child.'

'They're an acquired taste. And?'

'And what?' She was teasing, flirting, and loving it. She hadn't acted this way for so long, hadn't been this relaxed since—for ever.

'And what other things are you thinking?' Jace asked softly.

'What you're thinking,' Eleanor returned, and Jace smiled.

'I'm thinking how lovely you look tonight,' he said. 'And how jealous I am of that necklace.'

Eleanor touched the snowflake pendant that nestled between her breasts and blushed.

'So tell me what you've been doing these last ten years besides work,' Jace said, dispelling the sudden tautening moment, and, a little disappointed, Eleanor picked up her fork.

'Not much, really,' she said, spearing her last bite of baklava. 'Work has been my life, more or less.'

'And are you happy like that?' Jace asked quietly.

'Are you?' Eleanor returned. 'Because, based on your private jet and island and who knows what else, I'm guessing that work has pretty much been your life too.'

She heard the challenge in her voice, felt it in her soul, and yet it rushed out of her when Jace replied softly, 'No. I don't think I am.'

'Oh.' Eleanor sat back in her chair. 'Well, neither am I, I suppose,' she admitted. It was the first time she'd ever said it aloud. It was the first time she'd even let herself *think* it.

'So what would you like to do, if you could do anything?' Jace asked as he took a sip of wine. 'Not open a bakery, I guess.'

'Well…' Eleanor glanced down at her plate, suddenly shy. She hadn't expected Jace to ask so many questions; she hadn't expected to tell him so much. Yet somehow, strangely, it was easy. 'I had this dream—a daydream, really—about opening a non-profit foundation. I do love planning parties, and I've—dreamed—about doing it for charity. For sick kids or poor kids who can't afford or arrange a party of their own.' She looked up, smiling wryly. 'I don't know if it's even possible, but I like the thought of providing something fun—frivolous, even—for children who can never experience that.' And then, even though it had been easy to tell him, Eleanor suddenly found her throat becoming tight and her vision blurred. She looked back down at her plate and swallowed hard. She couldn't tell Jace more than that, or just why that dream was so precious. She'd told him enough already.

She felt the warmth of Jace's hand as he covered her own. 'That sounds like a very worthwhile dream.'

'Thanks.' She cleared her throat and risked looking up. 'What about you? What would you like to do with your life, if you could do anything?'

Jace sat back in his chair; Eleanor missed the warmth and security of his touch. 'I don't know. I've been so focused on building my business—making money—that I've never thought of doing anything else.'

'And it's not as if money is a concern,' Eleanor said lightly. 'You could do anything you wanted to, Jace.'

His lips twitched and from the warm gleam in his eyes Eleanor was suddenly quite sure he wasn't thinking about business. And neither was she. 'Mmm. That's an intriguing thought.'

'It is, isn't it?' she agreed shakily. Jace's gaze didn't leave hers as he drew his napkin from his lap and tossed it on the table. 'I think we're done with dinner.'

'Yes…' Eleanor whispered. Waiting.

Slowly, silently, Jace took her hand and drew her up from the table. Still without speaking he led her back into the villa, now washed in moonlight. Eleanor's heart hammered and her throat turned dry but still she followed him without a protest. Without a word.

When she saw he was leading her to his bedroom—not hers—she gave an involuntary little gasp, no more than a breath of sound, but Jace turned around to look at her, his face a question. 'Eleanor?' he asked, and she simply nodded.

Yes.

CHAPTER TEN

JACE opened the door. His bedroom was cloaked in darkness, but in the glimmer of moonlight Eleanor made out the huge shape of a king-sized bed, the sheen of a satin duvet. Jace turned to face her, and her breath caught. He looked so intent, so intense, so…reverent. And so beautiful.

She realised then just how much she wanted this. Had been waiting for this. Even so, a flutter of fear forced her to admit, 'It's been a long time…for me.'

'Me too, actually,' Jace replied, and Eleanor heard the smile in his voice.

'Really?' She couldn't keep the disbelief from her own voice. Somehow she'd imagined that Jace had been enjoying countless easy and meaningless love affairs in the last ten years while she'd had only a handful of failed relationships.

'Really,' he confirmed, one eyebrow lifting in irony. 'And just why would you think otherwise?'

She shrugged, unable to admit that when he'd left her she'd painted him as a womaniser, a user. It had made her own loss more bearable. She was still holding onto what she'd once believed—assumed—about him, rather than what she really knew. What she was beginning to believe.

'I don't know,' she admitted softly. 'Maybe it's because I can't imagine any woman resisting you.'

'I only care about one woman,' Jace replied, his voice as soft as hers, 'and she's been quite accomplished at resisting me.' His voice caught, and Eleanor heard the vulnerability. 'I only hope she doesn't resist me now.'

'She won't,' she whispered, and Jace drew her to him, cupping her face in his hands as he kissed her with a sweetness that left Eleanor fulfilled and aching at the same time.

He pulled away, and she saw the glimmer of his smile, the flash of his teeth in the darkness, as he led her to the bed. Nerves fluttered through her once more. She was ten years older and probably ten pounds heavier than the last time they'd been together. She might look killer in a business suit, but naked? She had *stretch marks*.

And Jace looked just amazing. That belief was confirmed as he shrugged out of his shirt, his chest gleaming in the moonlight. He reached for the zip of her dress, and in one simple, sensual tug he pulled it all the way down to her waist. Eleanor shrugged, instinctively, and the dress slithered to the floor. She caught her breath, waiting as Jace gazed at her; she wore only her bra and underwear.

'You are beautiful,' he whispered. 'And I've waited a long time for this.'

'So have I,' Eleanor whispered back, a laugh lurking in her voice. Smiling, Jace slipped her bra straps from her shoulders. Within seconds she was naked, struggling between self-consciousness and a confidence she wasn't sure she really felt. Yet when Jace reached out one hand and with his fingertips gently traced a path down her body from her collarbone to her hip she felt as if he were memorising the map of her body, as if he were treasuring it. And she relaxed.

Even better, Jace shrugged out of the rest of his own clothes so he stood there, magnificent and naked, before leading her to the bed. The satin duvet was slippery on her skin until Jace peeled it back, stretching out beside her so their bodies just barely touched. The only sound was their breathing. Carefully, cautiously, Eleanor laid a hand on Jace's chest. His skin was warm. God help her, she was so nervous. So afraid. And yet still so happy. It was a strange, unsettling mix of emotions.

'Don't be afraid,' Jace whispered. He brushed a strand of hair away from her face, dipping his head so his lips were inches from her. 'We don't have to do this.'

Eleanor felt the plunging sensation of deep disappointment. 'Oh yes, we do. You're not running away now.'

'I'm not moving,' Jace assured her. His lips grazed her ear, her jaw, and Eleanor shuddered. 'I'm not going anywhere,' he promised.

Eleanor closed her eyes as his lips moved from her jaw to her neck to her breast, and she added silently, *Not ever.*

Conversation became improbable after that, and then impossible. The exquisite sensation of being, not only cherished, but also possessed forbade all speech or even thought. Jace moved over her, teasing, treasuring as Eleanor's slick fists bunched on his back, her nails digging into his skin as he kissed his way up and down her body, taking his time in the most sensitive places.

Then, when Eleanor thought she could bear it no more, he rolled over so she was on top of him, his erection pressing insistently against her stomach as he looked up at her and smiled. 'Your turn.'

'My—turn?' Now she was shy. Now she had control. Slowly Eleanor lowered her head and kissed his chest. She remembered this, remembered how good it had once been between them. It had been so long, but she remembered. She moved lower, gaining confidence as she heard Jace's moan of pleasure.

Then, before she could move to the very heat and heart of him, he flipped her over and with a low growl said, 'All right. Now it's *both* of our turns.'

He entered her in one sweet, smooth stroke, and Eleanor closed her eyes, felt the surprising sting of tears behind her lids. This was so good. So right. To know and be known. To be as one.

One. One *person.*

That was how it felt in this moment of sweet union, the connection between them more intense and powerful than it had ever been, wiping away ten years of history, ten years of memories and sorrow and pain. This was more. This was better.

This really was starting over. Something new, something new and good and pure.

Afterwards they lay silently, Eleanor in the circle of Jace's arm, her head on his shoulder. She drifted her hand across the taut skin of his abdomen, half amazed at how comfortable she already was with his body.

'You know,' Jace said quietly, 'we didn't use protection.' Instinctively Eleanor stiffened, and Jace felt it, his arms tightening around her. 'I've never thought I had to ask this before, but is there any chance you could become pregnant?'

Such a simple question. So honest, so blunt, so basic. Eleanor swallowed. 'No,' she said quietly, her throat tight, 'there isn't. It's—taken care of. I'm on the pill.'

Jace nodded, saying nothing, and Eleanor was too afraid to ask. Did he *want* a baby, now he thought it might be a possibility? He'd implied before that his fertility wasn't a concern, yet how could it not be? How could it not be a consuming desire?

Her throat was tight, too tight, and the sleepy, sated feeling that had been stealing through her now seemed to evaporate completely, leaving her tense and wide awake. She should say something, start explaining, yet she couldn't. She was too afraid to ruin this moment, to ruin everything.

She closed her eyes, her throat still tight, the emotion too near the surface, seeping through.

'Eleanor?' Jace queried softly. She knew he could sense her sorrow. She just shook her head, unwilling to speak. In response Jace pulled away a little, but it was still too much. Her eyes were still closed, but she knew he was looking at her. Examining her. Then, with one gentle finger, he traced the silvery line of one of the stretch marks that ran along the inside of her hip. His voice, when it came, was no more than a husky murmur. 'Tell me about our daughter.'

Eleanor let out a choked sob of surprise. *'Jace—'*

He bent his head and kissed that silver streak of skin, the badge of her motherhood that never was. 'Tell me,' he whispered, but Eleanor knew it was a command. She knew he deserved to know. And, surprisingly, amazingly, she realised she wanted to tell him.

In actuality it was easy. She'd been dreading this conversation for days, weeks, *years*, but now that it was here, that Jace had asked, the words spilled from her lips. No one else knew. No one else had been there.

'She was beautiful,' she whispered. *'Beautiful.'* Jace didn't speak, but she felt the welling of his own emotional response, the swell of sorrow he must now feel that she had been living with for ever. 'Perfect,' she added. 'And I don't just mean the usual ten fingers, ten toes. Her face was like a little rosebud. A folded up, unfurled rosebud.' Eleanor could still see the closed eyes, the pursed lips. God, it hurt.

Jace's hand found hers. He squeezed her fingers tight, hard, almost hurting, and Eleanor welcomed the touch. *Touch me,* she silently commanded. *Hold me. Don't ever let me go. Not now, especially not now.*

'What happened?' he finally whispered. Eleanor shook her head, her eyes still clenched shut.

'It was her heart. It had a defect and it just—stopped. Like a clock winding down. Nothing else was wrong. She was perfect in every way. But when I went for my six-month check-up, there was no heartbeat.' She drew in a ragged breath. 'They said it happens sometimes with the Dopplers, they can't find the heartbeat. They told me not to worry— yet.' Jace squeezed her hand harder, and Eleanor squeezed back, holding on, needing him now as her anchor. 'So I had an ultrasound. I saw her there on the screen, all curled up, unmoving. Silence.' The room had echoed with it. She drew in another breath, the sound a desperate gasp. 'So I had to be induced. Like labour. Like birth—only, it wasn't. It was the hardest, loneliest thing I've ever done.'

'Was your mother there? Or a friend?'

'No. My mother was in California on a business trip and couldn't get back. And my friends were in college. This was totally out of their realm.'

'So you went through it alone? Eleanor, I'm sorry.' His voice was rough, his hand still clenched over hers.

'The thing that kept me going was knowing I would at least see her. Hold her in my arms. That would have to be enough.' She turned to him, her hand slipping from his to rest on his chest in an act of supplication. 'And I did, and she was beautiful, Jace, oh, God, she *was*—' And then the tears she'd been holding back for far too long finally fell, streaming down her cheeks in hot, healing rivers as Jace held her and rocked her silently.

Finally, after an eternity, she drew in a gulping breath and tried, if not to smile, at least to seem calm. And she did feel calm, now. 'I've never told anyone that before.'

'No one?'

She shook her head. 'It was easier not to. But you—you deserve to know.'

'Do I?' Eleanor heard the bitter note of recrimination in his voice. 'What a bastard I was. You never—never should have had to go through that on your own.'

'It's okay—'

'No,' Jace said savagely, 'it's not okay. I'll never accept that it was.' He clasped her hands, still resting on his chest, in his, and gazed at her with tear-bright eyes. 'Forgive me, Eleanor, for what I did. For what I assumed. And most of all for how I failed you…in so many ways. I don't ever want to fail you again.'

Eleanor nodded jerkily. 'I forgive you,' she whispered, and this time she meant it and believed in it with all of her heart. When he'd asked in the park it had been too soon. She hadn't been able to let go, and Jace hadn't known enough. Now it was real. Now it was true.

Now it was good.

She rested her head against his chest, exhausted, emotionally drained, yet still sated and, surprisingly, happy. She knew there was more to say, and she felt then she had the strength to say it. Just not now. Not yet.

Jace gathered her in his arms, resting his chin on top of her head, and Eleanor felt as if she could happily stay like that all night or, even better, for ever.

He'd had no idea. No true idea of all the pain and heartache and grief he'd caused. Still holding Eleanor in his arms, Jace closed his eyes in bitter and desperate regret. He'd known he'd hurt her, but he'd had no idea of how much. No wonder she couldn't trust him.

Except now he thought she did, and the realisation terrified him. He wasn't ready for that kind of trust. He didn't know what to do with it.

He was afraid of failing.

What good are you? What use?

Jace closed his eyes. Gently he stroked Eleanor's tear-dampened hair, awed by the courage she'd shown in so many amazing and unbearable ways. She still had the sweetness of the woman he'd known ten years ago, but now with it she possessed a strength that humbled him.

Jace's heart contracted and he felt a tightness in his throat as Eleanor curled her body into his in an act more intimate than what they'd just done. She rested her head on his shoulder, her hair tickling his nose, and with a satisfied little sigh she slept.

When Eleanor awoke Jace was gone. She stretched sleepily before feeling the empty space next to her in the bed, feeling it in her heart. Her whole body went rigid. Where had he gone? Did he regret last night? She thought of all the things she'd done—*said*—and closed her eyes. She couldn't bear it if he regretted it.

'Good morning.'

She bolted upright, the sheet falling from her naked body. Jace sat in a chair across from the bed, his laptop opened on the coffee table next to him. He wore only a pair of jeans and his hair was a little mussed.

'Good morning,' Eleanor answered. She slipped back down under the sheet.

'I didn't want to disturb your sleep,' Jace told her, giving her that wonderful crooked smile, 'but I couldn't leave you either.'

'You couldn't?'

'No.' The word was a confession, and it was enough. Eleanor didn't want to test or examine anything; she just wanted to trust. Finally. She smiled, shyly, and Jace stood up, stretching out one hand towards her.

'Let's get some breakfast. I'm starving.'

'So am I,' she admitted and slipped from the bed.

The morning was touched by magic. When they came into the kitchen breakfast had already been laid and the aroma of fresh coffee filled the room, although Agathe was nowhere in sight. She had, it seemed, anticipated their every need and then tiptoed quietly away.

After a lazy hour or two of eating and talking—Eleanor couldn't believe how relaxed she felt—she decided she needed to do a little work at least.

She stretched and regretfully pushed away from the table. 'I should start planning this party.'

'We have time.'

'Jace, your father's party is in ten days. It takes time to order things, food—'

He shrugged, reaching for her hand. 'We still have time—'

'I need to think of a theme,' she insisted even as she let him slide his fingers along hers, his thumb finding her palm and brushing against it in a way that made her whole body faint with longing. 'I was wondering,' she continued, still determined to do some work, 'if you have any photos or things from your childhood. We could put them around—'

Jace's fingers tightened on hers for a tiny second. 'Why? This isn't my party.'

'No, but we're celebrating your father's life. Memories are important—'

'Are they?' he asked with a strange little smile and withdrew his hand.

Eleanor frowned. She knew Jace's relationship with his father must have been difficult at times; he'd indicated as much, especially in regards to his alleged infertility. Yet this was his *father*, and he was throwing a party for him. Would a photo or two really be unwanted? Resented, even?

Jace's face had gone strangely still, even blank, and Eleanor was left with the feeling that he was wearing a mask, just as she'd felt when he'd danced with her at the party. Except this was a different mask, a colder, crueller one, and she had no idea what emotion—what person—hid underneath. Even after last night and everything she had shared, she suddenly wondered if she still knew Jace…at all.

She pushed the thought away, not liking it. 'Do you have any better ideas?' she asked, lightly, and Jace shrugged.

'There is a box of old photographs up in one of the spare bedrooms. My sister Alecia had them and she didn't have room in her new flat, so she brought them here one visit. You can take a look through them, if you like.' He rose from the table, his face still ominously blank. 'If you're going to do some work, so should I. I'll see you at lunch?' Although it was a question, Jace didn't give her time to answer. Eleanor watched him stride from the room without a backward glance, and she felt his withdrawal—emotional and physical—like a coldness creeping into her bones and stealing over her soul.

She sat in the kitchen for a few minutes, listening as a door in the distance clicked firmly shut. She thought of all the things she'd said last night. What had Jace said? What had *he* shared?

Uncomfortably, painfully, she became aware of how one-sided last night had really been…how one-sided everything had been. It seemed *she* was the only one starting over.

Sighing, trying to push away her growing sense of

discouragement, she decided to find the photographs. She was used to immersing herself in work to stop the hurt. The fear. She could do it again, even if she was tired of it. Even if she didn't want to.

Upstairs she walked along the silent corridor, poking her head in empty bedrooms, peering in darkened cupboards until she finally came across a wardrobe filled with cardboard boxes. Hesitantly she pulled one out; a faded photograph fluttered to the ground and Eleanor stooped to get it. She studied the picture: five darling, dark-eyed girls, and a laughing little boy who had the same crooked smile she knew—and loved.

Loved. The word caught her by surprise. Did she love Jace? Did she know enough about him to love him? Eleanor tried to study the question from an objective, analytical standpoint, and failed. How could you be objective about love? She knew her heart raced when she saw him. She knew how treasured and cherished she felt in his arms. She knew how happy he made her feel, and how he always could make her laugh, even when she didn't want to.

Was that love? Was it real? Could it be enough?

There were so many things she didn't know about him. His secrets. His hopes. His fears. His favorite colour.

Purple.

Her lips twitched and a smile bloomed on her face, stirred in her heart. Perhaps she did know him enough. Perhaps you didn't need to know someone's whole history to love him. And, Eleanor thought as she opened the box she pulled out, perhaps she could find out some of the things she didn't know. Yet.

She spent the rest of the morning and a good part of the afternoon gazing at a lifetime of photos. Birthday parties, Christmas dinners, lazy summer days on the beach, from round-cheeked babies to curly-haired toddlers, the scraped knees of early childhood to the gangly insecurity of adolescence. She saw Jace's early life documented in snapshots, from a laughing little boy to a solemn-eyed youth whose expression looked…haunted. Gazing at those photos, Eleanor guessed Jace must have been about fifteen. He would have already had mumps. He would have learned of his own infertility. She could see the struggle and the sorrow in every taut line of his adolescent face.

And yet the man she'd known in Boston, the student she'd fallen in love with, had been young and laughing and seemingly carefree. Had that been a façade, just as it had been the night of the party? A pretence, to cover the pain? She knew all about that.

'I see you've found them.'

Eleanor's head jerked up and she saw Jace lounging in the doorway. From the long shadows slanting across the floor, she figured she must have been in this room for hours. 'Yes,' she said. She glanced down at the photo of Jace she was still holding: a snap of him as a teen, his father standing behind him, his hand heavy on Jace's shoulder. Neither were smiling. 'Yes, I did.'

Jace ambled into the room. 'Let me see,' he drawled, reaching for the photograph. Eleanor gave it to him wordlessly. As Jace took it his face tightened, his eyes narrowing, and Eleanor's heart ached. She thought of how much that photo revealed, and yet how much it didn't say. How much she still didn't understand. 'Ah, yes,' he said as his gaze flicked over the photo before he handed it back to Eleanor. 'You might not want to put that one on display.'

Eleanor put it back in the box. 'Jace…tell me about it.'

'It?' he repeated, the single word not inviting questions.

Still Eleanor persevered. 'Your family. Your past. Your father.'

Jace hesitated, and Eleanor held her breath. *Tell me,* she implored silently. *Open up to me like I opened up to you.* That was what love was. To know and be known. Then he gave her a cool little smile and turned back to the door. 'There's nothing really to tell. Agathe's made dinner. You haven't eaten all day. You must be hungry.'

And leaving her with more questions—and more disappointment—than ever before, he left the room.

Jace walked quickly from the bedroom, from Eleanor. He felt restless, edgy, even angry. He didn't like the thought of her thumbing through those photos; he didn't like what they revealed. He didn't like Eleanor asking questions, wanting answers. What answers could he give? How could he tell her the truth? He didn't want her to know about his father's disappointment, how *he* had been such a disappointment.

He didn't want to be a disappointment to Eleanor.

Sighing, Jace raked a hand through his hair. Everything had been going so well. They'd both been so relaxed, so happy. Why did a few meaningless snaps have to ruin it? Why did these old feelings of fear and inadequacy have to swamp him, rushing through him in an unrelenting river as he looked through those photos, as he remembered every tiny sigh and little remark his father made, each one wounding the boy he'd been so deeply?

He wasn't that boy any more. He wasn't even infertile any more. Yet here he was, still mired by feelings of fear and inadequacy. It came to him then in a startling flash of insight that he wasn't just afraid of hurting Eleanor; he was afraid of being hurt himself.

That was what caring—love—did to you. It opened you up, it left you open and exposed, raw and wounded.

And yet it was—it could be—the best thing to ever happen to him…if he let it.

He just didn't know if he could.

As he retreated to his office, burying his thoughts and his fears with paperwork and business deals, he wondered if perhaps the past couldn't truly be forgotten. Perhaps you could never escape the old memories, fears, failures. Perhaps you couldn't start over after all.

By the time Eleanor had cleaned herself up and arrived downstairs for dinner, any remnant of the darkness and anger she'd felt from Jace upstairs had vanished. Instead he was his usual relaxed, carefree self, smiling readily, chatting easily, pouring her wine—yet Eleanor didn't trust any of it.

Now her mind seethed with questions, and they made her heart hungry and restless. Why was Jace holding back now, when she'd given him nearly everything? Was he regretting the night they'd shared, the secrets *she'd* shared? She still felt painfully conscious that he hadn't shared anything, that he was keeping himself distant and remote and *safe*, and it scared her.

Yet after dinner, when Jace led her upstairs, she didn't have the strength or even the desire to protest. Eleanor's heart bumped against her ribs and her fingers tingled where he'd laced them through his, pulling her along gently.

'Jace—'

'Is something wrong?' he murmured, lifting his free hand to brush it against her cheek. Eleanor leaned her face into the cup of his palm as a matter of instinct, a decision of need. She didn't just want him any more; she needed him. She couldn't fight this, and she didn't even want to, not for something so nebulous as a few haunted memories. Didn't she have those too?

You told them to Jace. He's keeping them from you.

She pushed the thoughts—and the fears—away and, smiling softly, followed him into the bedroom.

CHAPTER ELEVEN

THE next week followed the same pattern. When they weren't working—Jace on his business and Eleanor on the party— they were enjoying each other's company, in bed as well as out of it, but Jace still seemed distant to Eleanor, withdrawing more each day. His heart felt hidden, and she didn't know how to find the true him, the man she thought she loved.

Every question she asked that would make him talk about himself he deflected with a joke or a question back at her, and Eleanor realised how, in all the time she'd known him, he'd never really talked about himself. He'd never been vulnerable, or emotional, or even real, the way she had.

The inequality of it made her feel even more exposed, and terribly uncertain. Perhaps, when these two weeks were over, she would go back to New York and Jace would return to Athens. Perhaps these two weeks were all they were ever meant to have. What had Jace said? *And whatever* this *is, maybe it will go somewhere, and maybe it won't.* It was so little, Eleanor thought now. So very little, and yet she'd accepted it, fallen into his hand with the ease of a ripe peach. And that was what she felt like: something to be plucked, enjoyed, and then discarded.

With the party only a week away, Eleanor was forced to push aside her own personal concerns for the far more pressing one of the upcoming event. She'd made preliminary orders for food, and booked a band from Naxos, but she still felt she lacked the key idea that would bring this party together, that would give it both a theme and a heart.

And Jace wasn't helping at all.

'Does your father have any favourite foods?' she asked one afternoon. She'd sought Jace out in his office, and now he barely looked up from his laptop as she waited for his answer. Last night they'd made love—at least it had felt like love—but now Eleanor thought they seemed like strangers.

'I really don't know.'

Eleanor sighed impatiently. 'What about music? Games? Activities? Help me out here, Jace. This is your father's party.'

Jace looked up, his lips pressed together, his eyes flashing. 'And, as you can probably see for yourself, I never knew my father very well. We've barely talked in fifteen years.'

Eleanor's mouth dropped open as shock raced icily through her. She'd guessed their relationship was strained, but this? Utterly estranged?

'Why, Jace? And why on earth are you having the party here if that's—'

He shrugged, the gesture one of dismissal. 'If you need details, you can ring my sister Alecia. The party was her idea—she can tell you what you need to know.'

Eleanor bit back the retort that he might have volunteered this information several days ago; she didn't want to argue. And even though they hadn't had an argument, precisely, she left the room feeling disgruntled and unhappy and heartsore.

Up in her room she reached for the phone and dialled the number Jace had given her. After a few rings a bright, cheerful voice answered.

'Kalomesimeri.'

Eleanor scrambled for the basic Greek phrases she'd learned in the last week. Fortunately, most people she'd dealt with had spoken English. She hoped Jace's sister was the same. *'Kalomesimeri... Mi la te Anglika?'*

'Yes, I certainly do,' Alecia replied, her voice warm with laughter. 'And you sound American.'

'Yes. My name is Eleanor Langley, and I'm planning your father's birthday party.'

'An American planning the party! How original of Jace. And I suppose he's not being helpful at all, and sent you to me?'

'That's it exactly,' Eleanor said in relief, and Alecia gave a gurgle of laughter.

'Typical Jace. So busy with his precious work. He wasn't always like this, you know.'

'No,' Eleanor agreed, then realised Alecia would have no idea she had a history with Jace. She didn't particularly want to share that information, either. 'No?' she said again, this time a question.

'No, he was quite fun in his youth,' Alecia replied dryly. 'But I suppose everyone must grow up. What is it you want to know?'

'I'd love some details about his—your—father. I found some photographs, but—'

'Oh, yes, I dropped those off ages ago.'

'Well, what is your father like?' Eleanor asked. 'And what kind of party would he like? I've been trying and—'

'Oh, you don't need anything fancy,' Alecia assured her. 'My father grew up on the docks of Piraeus. He was a street rat, and he worked his way up to what he is now. He can't stand anything ostentatious or ornate...he likes things plain. And he speaks plainly too. He can be a grumpy old bear sometimes, to tell the truth, but I know he loves us all.'

Silently Eleanor wondered if Jace knew that as well. From everything she'd witnessed so far, she doubted it. 'All right,' she said slowly, still wondering just what kind of party she could put together.

'He loves old rembetika music,' Alecia told her. 'You know the street music with guitars? He grew up on it, and he's not ashamed of his past.'

'Rembetika,' Eleanor repeated. She reached for her notebook.

'But, you know, the main reason for the party is for us to be all together as a family,' Alecia continued, her voice turning serious. 'We haven't been together properly in years—one of my sisters is usually off having a baby, or Jace can't make it because of work. Having everyone together will be the most important thing about the party—that's what really matters.'

'I see,' Eleanor said. She wondered how Alecia could speak about her father in such a warm, loving way when Jace's experience was obviously so different.

'Of course, you must have tarama salata—fish-roe salad—and loukomia, a kind of jellied sweet. They are his favourites.'

'Tarama, loukomia,' Eleanor repeated, scribbling madly. 'Thank you.'

Armed with this new information, she set about arranging orders, finding a provider of the aforementioned food, and ringing up the band in Naxos to ask if they played rembetika. She still felt utterly out of her depth, and, combined with the sudden alienation she felt from Jace, it made her feel more like a lonely stranger than ever.

'How's it going?' Jace asked that evening as Eleanor pored over her notes spread across the kitchen table. Jace had skipped dinner, claiming work, and Eleanor had eaten with Agathe. She'd barely seen him all day, and now the moon was high in the sky, casting its lambent light across the smooth surface of the sea.

'Fine,' Eleanor replied a bit shortly. 'Your sister had some good information.'

'Good.' They both fell silent, the tension tautening between them. Eleanor turned back to her notes. 'Come to bed,' Jace said finally, his voice a lazy murmur.

She looked up, saw Jace's sleepy smile, and knew he wanted to solve everything with sex. And it would be so easy to say yes; God only knew, her body wanted to. She felt longing uncoil sinuously within her as Jace stretched out his hand.

'No, Jace.' He stilled, wary, and Eleanor shook her head. 'I...I need to work for a little while longer. The party is in just a few days.'

'Fine.' He dropped his hand, and Eleanor saw a new coolness creep into his eyes, harden the planes and angles of his face. Without another word he turned and left the room.

An hour later she came to her own bed, not Jace's, and crept into it alone. Half of her wanted to find Jace, or have him find her, yet she knew neither would solve what was—and wasn't—between them. She needed more than what they found together in bed, good as that was. She needed honesty, yet she was too much of a coward to ask for it.

The next morning when Eleanor came into the kitchen Jace was already there. In a business suit. His briefcase rested against the leg of his chair. Eleanor's stomach plunged icily, right down to her toes. Jace looked up from the newspaper he'd been scanning.

'Good morning.'

'Are you leaving?' Eleanor blurted, hating how afraid she sounded.

'I need to go to Athens for a short business trip,' Jace replied smoothly. 'I'll be back for the party.'

'For the *party*? You're leaving me here until the party?' She hadn't expected *that*. She hadn't expected Jace to run away again.

'I'll be back before the party,' Jace explained, and Eleanor heard a bite of impatience in his voice. 'Surely you don't need me to help plan it? I wasn't being much help, as far as I could tell.'

'No, you weren't,' Eleanor agreed, sitting opposite him. She reached for the coffee pot, then pulled her hand back. Her fingers were trembling, and she didn't trust herself to hold it. She didn't trust herself at all. 'But I didn't expect you to *leave*—' Her voice caught, and she swallowed. 'What's going on, Jace?'

He didn't answer for a moment. Eleanor looked up at him, saw his expression was guarded, wary. 'Nothing,' he finally said. 'I told you, I have some business to attend to. I'll try to wrap it up as quickly as I can.' He turned back to his newspaper, conversation clearly over.

Frustration, disappointment, and fear all warred within her, bubbling up. 'And when you come back?' Eleanor asked evenly. 'What's going to happen then, Jace? Just what is between us?'

He looked up from his paper. 'I know there are things that need explaining between us,' he said slowly. 'We're both still figuring out what's going on—and what we want.'

Eleanor nodded jerkily. It all sounded so nebulous, so nothing. 'And?'

'And I think we can have that conversation when I return,' Jace finished. 'When the party is over, and we're both more relaxed.' He glanced at his watch. 'I have an eleven o'clock meeting this morning. I should go.' He rose from the table, and Eleanor just watched him numbly. She could hardly believe he was going, that he was leaving her here alone.

'Eleanor,' Jace said quietly. He reached out and gently— so gently—touched her cheek. 'This isn't the end.' Before Eleanor could respond or even process that statement, he'd picked up his briefcase and was gone.

As she heard the front door open and then click softly but firmly shut she realised she didn't believe what Jace had said. This certainly *felt* like the end.

There had been no real reason to go to Athens. Jace knew that, and the knowledge ate at him as he flew across the Aegean Sea, azure blue flooding his senses from both above and below. He was running away…again.

Yet he couldn't stay with Eleanor, couldn't bring himself

to give her what she needed—honesty, trust, *love*—until he had figured out what he was going to do. If anything was possible.

If *they* were possible.

Yet if he'd thought he might clear his head away from the island and Eleanor, he was completely mistaken. The doubts and fear seethed through his mind, tormenting him here just as they had at the villa.

I'll disappoint her. I won't be enough. She'll hurt me.

Wasn't that what he was afraid of? Hurt? Opening himself up to the pain and beauty of love? He was a coward, a frightened little boy. *Life* was pain. Life was hope.

And, burying himself in work, he'd avoided truly living for far too long.

His intercom buzzed, startling him from his thoughts.

'Alecia is here,' his assistant said, and Jace sighed wearily.

'Send her up.'

'I heard you were in Athens,' Alecia said as she breezed into the room, airily trailing shopping bags. Jace stifled a groan. He loved his sister, but he didn't particularly feel like seeing her now. Alecia was far too astute.

'How did you hear that?'

'I rang that American party planner of yours and she told me,' Alecia said as she sprawled in the chair across from Jace's desk. 'She sounded terribly gloomy, Jace. Are you sure she can pull off this party?'

'Absolutely.'

Alecia's eyes narrowed and she leaned forward. 'You have quite a lot of faith in her, don't you? Where did you meet this paragon?'

'She planned a party for me in New York,' Jace replied, shuffling some papers on his desk. He could feel his cheeks warm, damn it.

'New York…' Alecia repeated thoughtfully. 'And I *did* say you've been so grumpy since you came back from there…'

'Whatever it is you're thinking, Alecia—'

'It is a woman, isn't it? It's this—Eleanor. Another American.' She shook her head, even though she was smiling gleefully. 'Well, I hope she treats you better than—'

'Don't.'

'Oh, Jace.' Alecia leaned forward. 'You know we're the last holdouts for marriage and babies and all that. I'd love to find Mr Right, of course I would, but sometimes I think I'd rather you found your Princess Charming.'

Jace's mouth twitched. 'I didn't know there was such a person.'

'You know what I mean. It's not good to be alone. And I'd love to see you settled with a wife and babies—a little girl with your eyes—'

Pain pierced Jace's shell, the armour he'd been building around his heart. He'd had a daughter. Maybe she'd had his eyes. He'd never know. 'I don't know if that's in store for me, Alecia,' he said quietly. Even if it was possible.

'Why not? Why shouldn't you have a family of your own, a family to love?'

A family. The word caught Jace by surprise, on the raw. He felt his thoughts tumble and slide, for ever shift. A family. Not a child, an heir, a dynasty. Not a thing to be obtained, a possession, a means to an end, the way his father had seen a son, a grandson.

A *family*.

In that moment he could picture it so clearly, so beautifully. He saw himself, he saw a baby, he saw *Eleanor*, and all the fear fell away.

This was what he wanted. What he needed.

He loved Eleanor. It was suddenly so obvious, so overwhelming. It wasn't a possibility or a fear or a hope. It was *real*. His love. His family.

'Yes,' he said slowly, starting to smile. 'A family.'

For the next few days Eleanor immersed herself in work. She was good at that, good at using it to push her thoughts and fears away. Yet overseeing food deliveries and arranging catering still left her with far too much time to remember how good it had been between her and Jace, and wonder whether it really was over. He didn't call, and although she had his mobile number she wasn't quite desperate enough—yet—to ring him, when he obviously had no interest in speaking with her.

The afternoon before the party Eleanor was in the kitchen, going over sleeping arrangements of all the guests with Agathe, when her mobile phone finally trilled tinnily. Eleanor reached for it with a sense of relief; she'd been waiting for Jace to call all this time, even if she'd pretended—to herself—that she wasn't.

'Jace?'

'Hello, Eleanor.' His voice sounded warm, and even happy, and Eleanor felt it reverberate all through her body. She closed her eyes in relief. It was going to be okay. She hoped. 'How's the party planning going?'

'Good, I think. The party is tomorrow, you know,' she added, trying to sound light but not quite able to keep the edge from her voice. 'Your family is arriving all throughout the day. When are you coming home?' Home. She should have said *back*. Maybe this wasn't home; maybe *she* wasn't home.

'I'll be back tonight. I'm sorry I was delayed. I was waiting on something.'

'Waiting on something?' Eleanor repeated, wishing she had just a little bit more information, a little bit more insight into Jace's mind.

'I'll tell you everything tomorrow,' Jace said. 'I promise.'

Yet as Eleanor hung up the phone she knew she had no idea what *everything* was. What he'd been doing for the last few days, or the secrets of his heart that he'd been keeping from her.

Disconsolately she turned back to the to-do list she'd left on the table.

* * *

Jace hung up the phone, smiling. He knew Eleanor felt uncertain and confused and perhaps even afraid, but if she could hold on for one more day—if he could—then he knew everything would work out. Everything would be perfect.

Amazing, how his doubts and fears had fallen away in light of that one word, that one great truth: family.

For years he'd simply seen his infertility as his inability to sire a child, to please his own father. He hadn't considered—hadn't let himself consider—what it really meant. What he'd really been missing. And now that it could be a reality, now that the floodgates of his heart had finally opened, he knew exactly what he wanted. A family, with the woman he loved. Eleanor.

Love had been such a scary word, a terrifying idea. Love meant you let people in, and once you did they held the power to hurt you. Hurt him the way his father had, the way Eleanor had—or he'd thought she had. He hadn't ever wanted to experience that again, and so for ten years he hadn't let anyone in. He hadn't let anyone even close.

Yet now he was ready; he was more than ready. He was eager, excited, as giddy as a child. Tomorrow he would tell Eleanor he loved her. He would ask her to marry him and they would start their future together. He could see it all perfectly bright, shining and pure.

The day of the party dawned bright, hot, and clear. Eleanor gazed out at the flat, endless blue sky, devoid of a wisp of cloud, or the telltale streak of a jet. She hadn't heard Jace come back last night, even though she'd stayed up past midnight. She wondered if he'd returned at all.

Resolutely Eleanor turned away from the window. She still had a lot to do.

Yet when she came down into the kitchen, Jace sat at the table, drinking coffee and scanning the newspaper, looking wonderful. Eleanor's heart seemed to clamber right up into her throat.

'Jace—' she managed. She felt a smile spread across her face.

'Good morning.' He turned, his eyes warm as his gaze swept over her. 'I came in so late last night, I didn't want to disturb you.'

She nodded, swallowing. 'I'm just glad you're here.'

'As am I.' He paused, and Eleanor suddenly had the feeling that he was going to say something important, maybe even something wonderful, and her heart began to beat with a fast, unsteady rhythm. Then he smiled and said, 'I just heard that my sister Parthenope will be arriving with her brood in just a few minutes. But...we need to talk. There are things I want to tell you.'

Eleanor nodded mechanically. 'Okay.' What things? she wanted to ask. Demand. Good things? Jace rose from the table and came towards her. He brushed an unruly strand of hair from her face and then bent to kiss her. His lips were cool and soft.

'I have so much to say to you,' he said, and it felt like a promise. Eleanor made herself believe it was.

Jace's family arrived throughout the day, throngs of children and five glamorous sisters who possessed the same ink-black hair and grey eyes that he did. Eleanor greeted them all, trying to keep their names straight, smiling politely and nodding her head, all too aware that to them—to anyone—she was nothing but a stranger to fade into the background. The party planner. As far as they were concerned, she had no importance or relationship with Jace at all. And Jace was kept busy with the demands of his family so that Eleanor wondered if that was indeed all she had become. The very fact that she didn't know, that she might have handed Jace Zervas her heart again only for him to break it, was more than aggravating. It was agonising.

By mid-afternoon the party was in full swing, although Jace's parents hadn't arrived. Children played on the beach and climbed on the deckchairs while their parents lounged around, talking and laughing. Eleanor went from room to room, making sure there was enough food and drink, that everyone was happy. Jace was surrounded by his sisters, although Eleanor saw him beckon her over several times. She ignored it out of some perverse sense of duty, and also because she wasn't sure she wanted to hear how Jace introduced her.

This is my indispensable party planner...

'You've done such a wonderful job.' Alecia found her in the foyer, straightening the collection of photos she'd retrieved from upstairs and arranged in a display that highlighted what looked like the happiest moments of the Zervas family. Eleanor turned from the photos. 'Thank you.'

'My father will be so pleased, when he arrives.'

'Do you know when that will be?'

Alecia gave a little laugh. 'Who knows? Soon, I hope. He's like Jace, works all the time. Those two are really far too alike.'

'Are they?' Eleanor murmured, and Alecia cocked her head.

'How did Jace hire you?' she asked, and Eleanor heard suspicion. 'An American is really an unusual choice.'

'We're—acquaintances,' Eleanor prevaricated, and a feline smile curled Alecia's mouth.

'Acquaintances? Because I was quite sure when I saw Jace a few weeks ago that he'd met a woman. And when I suggested he hire someone to plan this party, he brightened considerably.' She pursed her lips, gazing at Eleanor with open speculation. 'I wonder if you know anything about that?'

Eleanor flushed. She was not about to reveal the intimacies of her relationship with Jace, not when she still had no idea what the future could possibly hold. 'I'm not sure,' she hedged.

The front doors of the villa were suddenly flung open, freeing her from a more detailed reply.

Aristo Zervas stood in the doorway, tall and imposing, the same steely eyes as Jace's sweeping over the room—and his family—with a cold assessment. His wife, Kalandra, her dark hair streaked with grey and her face wreathed in a welcoming smile, held onto his arm.

'Papa!' Alecia hurried towards her father, enveloping him in a hug, which he returned stiffly. Two of Jace's other sisters, Parthenope and Elana, followed suit. Jace, having entered the hallway upon his father's arrival, didn't move. Eleanor could feel the tension thrumming through him; she felt it in herself. It was as if they were waiting for a storm to break.

'Jace.'

Jace inclined his head. 'Father.' He drew himself up. 'There's someone I want you to meet.'

It felt unreal when Jace reached for her, a dream, as his arm curved around her waist. 'Father, this is Eleanor Langley.'

Aristo moved towards them. His silver gaze turned on Eleanor, took her in from her toes to the top of her head in one arctic sweep. Jace's arm tightened around her protectively. 'She is very important to me, Father.'

'Is she?' The corner of Aristo's mouth twitched up in what could be a smile or a sneer. Still spinning in shock, Eleanor managed to find her voice.

'It's nice to meet you, sir.'

Aristo nodded gruffly, then turned back to his son. 'So you were able to come to my party. Not working for once.' He paused, meaningfully. 'I don't know why you work so hard. Who are you going to pass it all on to?'

Eleanor flinched, the barb hurting her as well as Jace, although his face remained expressionless. He'd lived for years with remarks like that, she supposed. She felt nerves dance low in her stomach, a reminder that she hadn't told him everything. Yet when could she confess? What if it changed things? How could she *still* be such a coward, even now with Jace's arm around her, when he'd told his own father how he felt?

She is very important to me.

'The work is its own reward, Father,' Jace replied evenly. 'Now I'm sure you want to greet everyone else.' With a stiff nod, he drew Eleanor away from Aristo and everyone else crowding the foyer. Eleanor was barely aware of where he was going until they were on the terrace, and Jace tugged her towards the beach.

'Jace—the party—'

'They can do without us for a while. I've been trying to talk to you all day. I'd almost think you were avoiding me.'

'No—' Eleanor protested, half-heartedly, for she knew she had been avoiding him. Even now she was afraid, and it wasn't just because of what Jace might say, but what she *hadn't* said.

The sky was lavender, darkening to violet, the first stars visible on the horizon. Despite the lingering warmth of the sun, the wind that blew off the water was chilly. Eleanor kicked off her sandals as Jace led her across the beach; the sand under her feet was silky and cool.

'I'm sorry I didn't speak to you sooner.'

'It's all right.'

Jace turned back to her. The wind ruffled his hair and in the growing darkness Eleanor couldn't quite make out his expression. 'I'm sorry about my father as well. As you can see, we don't have a very close relationship.'

'Has it always been that way?' Eleanor asked.

'Ever since the mumps made me infertile.'

'Why would that affect your relationship so much?' Eleanor burst out. 'It wasn't your fault—you're still his son—'

He sighed and raked a hand through his hair. 'After five girls, my father's every hope was realised when I was born. I was the apple of his eye for the first fifteen years of my life—I still have those memories to hold onto.' He paused, and Eleanor thought he might stop, he might distance himself again as he'd done in the past. Then he continued more quietly, 'And my father's every hope dashed when I contracted mumps, and the doctor told him I would be infertile. All his life he'd worked hard building up an empire to pass onto his son, his son's sons. The Zervas dynasty.' He gave a short, humourless laugh. 'His dreams of a legacy—a dynasty—were destroyed that day. I was as good as useless. And he never let me forget it. And the damnable thing is, the doctor was *wrong*.'

Eleanor swallowed, her throat tight. 'Oh, Jace—'

'It doesn't matter any more.'

'But it does, of course it does—'

'No,' Jace corrected softly, 'it doesn't. I don't care what my father thinks of me, Eleanor. I'm not living my life to gain his approval, although perhaps I was doing that subconsciously by working so hard. Who knows?' He spread his hands wide. 'But when I went to Athens I realised what I wanted out of life.'

Her breath dried in her throat. 'What do you want?'

'You. I love you.'

Eleanor blinked back tears. She hadn't expected this; even now, when everything seemed so good, she hadn't expected so much. Honesty and love. Everything. 'I love you too,' she whispered.

'I went to Athens because I was scared,' Jace said. 'Everything was happening so fast, and I didn't know if I could handle it. I told myself I was afraid of hurting you, but I think I was really afraid of being hurt myself.'

'I know what that feels like,' Eleanor whispered.

'Ever since my father learned I was infertile, I felt like a failure to him, and in a way to everyone. I wasn't good enough on my own, just as a person. So I had ways of keeping people out. To keep from letting them in.' He gave her a crooked smile. 'I'd play the clown or just act like I didn't care. If you act like you don't care, perhaps you really won't.' Eleanor nodded, understanding, recognising those self-protective tendencies in herself, and Jace continued, his voice roughening with emotion, 'But that changed when I met you all those years ago. I let *you* in. With your kindness and your laughter and even your chocolate cupcakes. I couldn't help myself. And when I thought you'd lied to me—it hurt. So much. I was wrong, and yet I let that hurt fester inside me for years.' He shook his head in sorrowful acknowledgement of the years they'd lost. 'Then I found myself letting you in again, here on the island, and it scared me. I didn't want to be scared, but I was, and that's why I went to Athens. I needed to sort things out in my own mind—'

'And you did?' Eleanor broke in. 'You seem different now. More…sure.'

'I am.' Jace drew her to him, his hands smoothing the hair away from her face. 'I'm so sure, Eleanor. It was hell without you, even for just a few days, and it made me realise—actually my sister made me realise—'

He paused, laughing a little, and Eleanor prompted, 'Your sister?'

'Funny, the power of just one word. Family.' Eleanor shook her head, not understanding, and Jace reached for her hands. 'She told me she'd always wanted me to have a family, and I'd never thought of children that way before. I haven't thought of children at all for so long—I've even avoided my own nieces and nephews. But when I thought of my own inability to have children, it was simply as a failure. A disappointment to my father, to myself to provide an heir. To continue the dynasty. I never thought of it—of them—as a *family*.'

Jace was smiling, yet each word was a hammer blow to Eleanor's heart. Her throat was too tight to speak, so she just shook her head. She should have told him. Of course she should have told him. Why hadn't she? How could she have allowed it to come to this?

'But in that moment,' Jace continued, squeezing her hands, 'I realised what I wanted. What I've wanted all along, even though I've been fighting it. Love is scary, Eleanor. You know it as well as I do. Hope is dangerous.'

Oh, God help her, Eleanor thought numbly. So scary. *So* dangerous. She just shook her head, helplessly, as a tear slid down her cheek. In the darkness she didn't think Jace saw it.

'I want us to be a family, Eleanor,' Jace said softly. 'More than anything. And more than just that—I want us to spend the rest of our lives loving each other. I want to see you hold my son—or daughter, I don't care which. I never thought I could have it, I didn't even dare dream—but now I know it can be, and I want it all with you.' The moon slid from behind the clouds and in its silver rays Eleanor saw the tender, triumphant smile on Jace's face. She felt him slip his hands from hers as he dropped to his knee and fumbled in his pocket for what could only be a jewellery box.

'This is what delayed me an extra day in Athens. I wanted it to be perfect. It was my grandmother's, but I had the stone reset.' With a growing sense of unreality Eleanor watched as Jace stretched out his hand, flicking open the box. The moonlight glinted off the most amazing, enormous antique diamond she'd ever seen. 'Eleanor Langley, will you marry me?'

CHAPTER TWELVE

ELEANOR gazed at the ring, gazed at Jace and all the love shining in his eyes, and shook her head helplessly. 'Oh, Jace.'

'Is that a yes?'

'I never expected this,' she began, helplessly, for her mind was seething with disappointments and fears. She really *hadn't* expected this. She'd been living in the moment, enjoying Jace, loving him, yet her stupid, stubborn mind had pushed away any real thoughts of the future. Conveniently ignored the realities—the truths Jace had given her tonight. She'd wanted his honesty, yet now that she had it she realised it changed everything. For the worse.

'Eleanor?' Jace asked softly. 'What's wrong?' He stood up, reaching out to brush her damp cheek with one thumb. 'You're crying.'

'I'm overwhelmed.'

'That's okay.'

She nodded, jerkily, because it wasn't okay. It wasn't remotely okay. Of course Jace wanted children. A family. She'd been a blind fool, a willingly blind fool, not to see it—think it—before now. She hadn't wanted to think it. Hadn't wanted to be completely honest with Jace. She'd lacked—still lacked—the courage.

Jace wanted children—a family—and there was no way she could fit into that happy picture. Just as there was no way she could take that dream away from him now.

'Jace!' One of his sisters—Eleanor thought it was Parthenope—called from the terrace. She didn't understand the Greek, but the gist was all too apparent. They needed Jace back at the party.

'Photographs,' he explained tersely. 'I don't—'

'No. Go.' She shook her head, wiping her wet cheeks, and tried to smile. 'This is a party, Jace. We can talk—later.'

'Come with me. You should be in the photos—'

'No, no one even knows me yet. Besides, I need to check on the food. I'll see you later.' Already Eleanor was walking away from him, reaching for her sandals, not looking back.

'Eleanor,' Jace called, and she heard the frustration and confusion in his voice, sharpening her name. 'Whatever this is, it can be solved.'

Two more tears slid down her cheeks. Jace knew her, understood her so well. But he didn't know the most important thing, the thing she'd kept hidden. Shame roiled through her. All this time she'd been berating Jace for hiding his heart from her, yet now he'd been as honest and vulnerable as he could be, and she was the one who was still hiding. Who had been hiding all along, and who was still afraid. And some things couldn't be solved.

Jace smiled for photo after photo, his cheeks aching, as his gaze swept through the foyer. Where was Eleanor? She'd disappeared from the beach after his proposal—and that hadn't gone nearly as well as he'd expected.

In the moment when he'd shared that precious dream, Eleanor had looked devastated. And Jace had no idea why.

Frustration gnawed at him and as the photographer readied for yet another snap he broke away from the gathered crowd of his family.

'Jace,' Alecia protested, but he just shrugged as he strode away.

'I need to find Eleanor.' A feeling of foreboding stole over him as he walked through the empty rooms of the villa. He shouldn't have waited for so long.

* * *

Halfway to the kitchen the answer had presented itself, so apparent, so appalling. She needed to leave. She needed to leave *now*. If she stayed, she'd tell Jace the truth; he'd wrestle or coax it from her, and she didn't have the strength to resist. Then she would have to face the unbearable pain of his rejection, or, perhaps worse, the stoic acceptance of her own inadequacy. She couldn't do that to herself. She couldn't do it to Jace.

Yet she was on an island, and the only way off was Jace's private jet. Where could she hide? How could she escape? The questions pounded inside Eleanor's mind; she forced all other, more rational thoughts away.

Then Eleanor saw the lights of a farmhouse glimmering in the distance, heard the clank of a bell, and the answer came to her. *Of course.*

Hurrying upstairs to change into more serviceable clothes, she grabbed her purse and her passport—leaving everything else—and desperate, despairing, headed out into the night.

The track winding through the hills was lit only by a pale wash of moonlight, and Eleanor stumbled on the rocks and twisted tree roots. Even as she ran she knew she was being foolish. Yet she also knew she couldn't stay and watch Jace's dream be destroyed—or hers. She couldn't face him. She couldn't face the truth because it hurt too much.

Love hurt. Why had she risked it again after all these years? Why had she risked it with *Jace*?

After a quarter of an hour she found the farmhouse, huddled among the hills, and knocked on the door. Behind her somewhere a goat bleated.

The man who answered the door was grey-haired and a bit scruffy, a mug of coffee held in one hand. He stared at her blankly.

'*Yassas…parikalo…*' Every Greek word evaporated from her frazzled mind as she gazed at him helplessly.

'I speak English,' he told her, the words flat and a bit rough.

'Oh, thank God. I need to go to Naxos—on your boat—'

'At this hour?' He looked appalled.

'It's important—*please*.'

Something must have convinced him—the wildness in her eyes, or perhaps the ragged edge fraying her voice, or the wad of crumpled twenties she thrust at him. In any case, he shrugged, nodded, and said, 'I get my boots. It take twenty minute in the boat.'

Eleanor sagged against the doorway in relief.

A few minutes later they were on the beach, the sea no more than a sound in the darkness, the waves crashing onto the shore. The wind whipped Eleanor's hair into tangles, and she stared at the forlorn little rowboat dubiously. It really was small.

Good Lord, what was she *doing*?

'Is this the only boat?'

The farmer shrugged. 'The motorboat, it belong to Zervas.' He gazed at her speculatively, and Eleanor wondered how much he knew. How much he'd seen over the last few weeks.

For a moment—a second—she hesitated, wondering if she could go back to the villa and explain everything to Jace. Maybe he would understand. Maybe it would be okay. *Maybe.* She couldn't trust a maybe, she couldn't act on it. The fear that had taken root in her heart was too pervasive, twining its poisonous tendrils around every thought, every dashed hope.

She couldn't go back. She couldn't tell Jace the truth. She couldn't bear to see him disappointed, the dream he'd shared with her dashed, destroyed—

I want to see you hold my son—or daughter, I don't care which. I never thought I could have it, I didn't even dare dream—but now I know it can be, and I want it all with you.

Eleanor closed her eyes, a tiny sob escaping her. Her shoulders shook.

'You get in the boat?' The farmer held onto the edge of the boat with one work-roughened hand as the waves churned around him. Eleanor could hardly believe what she was doing, yet she was too afraid to face the other choices.

Coward. You're more of a coward than Jace ever was.

'Miss?'

'What the *hell* do you think you're doing?'

Eleanor froze. She felt a hand clamp down hard on her shoulder and whirl her around. Her purse slipped onto the sand. 'Jace—' She was glad to see him, even now, after everything. Glad and relieved, even though Jace looked livid. His angry gaze travelled from her to the man waiting with the boat. He spoke a few terse phrases of Greek and numbly Eleanor watched the man give a philosophical shrug before hauling his boat back onto the beach. Within seconds he was gone, swallowed up by the darkness.

Jace's gaze snapped back to her; his eyes were the colour of cold iron. 'So what is this?' he growled, his voice low and savage. 'Some kind of *revenge*?'

'Revenge?' Eleanor repeated blankly. Then her eyes widened and her heart squeezed painfully, robbing her of the ability to talk or even think—

'So I can see how it feels,' he sneered. 'Is that what this was all about, Eleanor? Coming to Greece, being with me, everything—' His voice tore and he pressed his lips together, his eyes flashing furiously.

He was *hurt*. She'd hurt him with her disappearance, of course she had. She'd hurt him more than the truth ever could.

She really was a coward.

'It's nothing like that, Jace,' she whispered, but he didn't look as if he'd even heard her. 'I swear to you, this wasn't revenge!' Her voice rose in a yelp as he pulled her along the beach, driven by his own fury and pain. 'Where are we—?' She stopped talking when she realised Jace was not in a mood to listen.

He led her away from the beach, back towards the villa, its

lights twinkling in the distance. Eleanor thought of facing all his family there and closed her eyes. She couldn't. 'Please,' she managed. 'Can't we just talk—alone?'

'Oh, yes,' Jace growled back at her. 'We are most certainly going to talk.'

Yet he didn't speak again until they'd reached the villa; he stalked past it, with Eleanor having no choice but to follow, her arm still in his strong grip.

'Where are we—?'

'Where do you think?' he snarled. 'Where you want to go.'

Eleanor didn't understand what he meant until she saw the dull gleam of his private jet under the moonlight.

'Jace—'

'Now.' He let go of her and she stumbled at the sudden release. The jet loomed in front of her, large and silent. 'I rang the pilot—he lives on Naxos. He should be here in a few minutes.'

Eleanor gazed at him, his face hard and implacable, his eyes two narrowed slits. 'Why—?'

'He can take you wherever you want to go. Back to New York, I presume.' He drew a breath, and it hitched. 'You didn't have to take a leaky rowboat in the middle of the night if you wanted to leave me, Eleanor. All you had to do was say.'

The look of naked pain on his face was too much for Eleanor to bear. She wrapped her arms around herself even though the wind wasn't that cold. What a mess everything was. What a mess *she'd* made. 'I don't want to leave you, Jace,' she whispered.

'Considering I found you trying to board a boat to Naxos without a single word of explanation, I find that hard to believe.'

'It's true.'

'So did it feel good? To leave me hanging, just as I did you? No word, no warning? Had you been waiting for this?' Each question was a laceration on her soul.

'*Stop*. I wasn't—I didn't mean—'

'Excuses!' Jace slashed a hand through the air. 'Well, get on the plane, Eleanor. Nothing is stopping you now.'

Anger made her straighten her shoulders and cross the tarmac to poke a finger in the hard wall of his chest. 'I'm not getting on that plane, Jace. Not yet, anyway. Yes, I ran away. But I didn't mean to leave you—it wasn't some kind of revenge—' Her voice broke on that horrible word, but she forced herself to go on. To confess the truth. 'It was fear. I was *scared*, Jace. I still am.' She dropped her hand and bowed her head, felt the sting of tears in her eyes.

Jace was silent for a long moment. 'What are you afraid of, Eleanor?' He didn't sound angry any more. He didn't sound particularly forgiving, either. Eleanor looked up. This was the hard part. This was why she'd run away in the first place.

'Afraid of disappointing you. Of you leaving me or staying with me for the wrong reasons—I'm not sure which would be worse.'

Jace's expression didn't change, didn't soften. 'Now it sounds like *you* don't trust *me*. Why would you disappoint me? Why would you think you could?'

She drew a breath and met his gaze directly. It hurt. 'Children, Jace,' she said rawly. 'I should have told you before. I meant to tell you—when we—that first night—' She swallowed, her throat so very tight. 'But I couldn't. I was too scared. And then everything was going so well, and I just stopped thinking about it because I wanted to be happy—for a little while—and you said you didn't even think about children very much—' She let out a hiccupy sob, knowing she wasn't making sense yet unable to speak the bald, bare truth.

Jace's face darkened, his mouth thinning. 'What are you saying?'

'I can't have children.' She saw the shock slice across his features, his mouth dropping open before he snapped it shut.

'What—how—?'

'It's not a fertility issue. I mean, I can *have* children, but—'
She closed her eyes. In her mind she saw the ominous, silent
screen of the ultrasound. Saw her baby's heart stilled for
ever. 'Our daughter had a heart defect. She was never going
to develop properly, never going to live. After—afterwards
I had some testing done.' She opened her eyes. 'It's genetic,
Jace. A genetic defect. A fluke, inexplicable, but there it is.
And the doctors said it's seventy-five per cent likely that
the same thing will happen again—with any pregnancy of
mine.' She swallowed past the aching tightness in her throat.
She couldn't bear to look at Jace now, so she gazed into the
distance, in the darkness. 'I can't live with those odds. I
can't—I can't go through it again. Not ever.'

Jace was silent for a long moment. Too long. Eleanor had
no idea what he was thinking, feeling. She didn't think she
could bear to know. She stared down at her feet, her vision
blurring. Somewhere she found her voice. 'I should have told
you, I know. I felt like you weren't being honest with me, but
I was the one who was hiding something. I'm sorry.' Jace
still didn't say anything, and it was the second time in her
life that silence had been such an endless agony. She drew a
long, shuddering breath and turned towards the plane. 'I…I
guess I'll go now.'

'Eleanor.' Before she could even move, Eleanor found
herself surrounded by Jace, his arms around her, pulling her
towards his chest. She was enveloped so her cheek rested
against the warmth of his neck, her body tucked wonderfully
into his. 'I'm sorry,' he whispered. 'I'm so sorry that you had
to go through that.'

'I'm sorry I can't—'

'I'm sorry too,' Jace whispered against her hair. 'I won't
pretend that I'm not, or that it doesn't hurt.' Eleanor swallowed a sob, and she felt Jace's fingers brush at the tears that
were sliding coldly down her cheeks. 'But, Eleanor, *Ellie*,
when I told you I wanted us to be a family… I wasn't—it's
more to me than just having a biological child. Yes, I expected

that, because I didn't know it was any different for you. But do I want a biological child—an *heir*—more than I want you? No. Never.' His arms tightened around her, drawing her closer to himself. 'God knows, my father drilled into me the utter importance of an heir, and it wrecked a good part of my life. Do you think I want to make that mistake again?'

Stunned, Eleanor couldn't answer. Couldn't think. She only hoped. Jace brushed the tangled curls away and cupped her face in his hands in a gesture so tender and achingly sweet that she couldn't keep the tears from slipping down her cheeks. He brushed at them with his thumbs.

'I was telling you I love you, Eleanor. *You*. All of you. Neither of us is perfect or even whole. We have scars. Memories. Regrets. But that's what love is. What it *does*. It takes everything—good and bad—and lives with it. Accepts it. Do you accept me with all *my* failings and mistakes?' He smiled crookedly, and Eleanor let out a sound that was half-laugh, half-sob.

'Yes.'

'And I accept you. I'm not walking away because of this. I'm not walking away at all.' He brushed his lips softly across hers. 'Not this time, and not ever.'

'But I don't want you to be disappointed,' Eleanor whispered, her throat still so very tight.

'Disappointed?' Jace's face seemed to crumple for a moment. He shook his head. 'I always felt my father was disappointed in me for not giving him what he wanted, the ability to continue our precious bloodline. I lived with that shame for years, and I don't think I ever escaped it until I met you. You made me feel whole. Happy. Like the man I was supposed to be, the man I wanted to be.'

'But if you want—'

'I want *you*. And I could never make any person—and especially you—feel that way. And I could never be disappointed in *you*. Yes, I'm disappointed that we won't have a child that is part of both of us, but that's something we can deal with together. I love you, Eleanor. I love your strength and your courage and your humour and your smile—everything. I love that you have drawn out the best in me, made me the man I want to be. No matter what, you couldn't disappoint me.'

Eleanor could hardly believe what he was saying. She wanted to trust it—with all her heart, she wanted to trust it—yet even so she still felt the lingering traces of fear.

'You told me—you wanted children. That's a big thing, Jace.'

'I want a family. Our family. And there are more ways than one to have children. We could adopt—do you want children, Eleanor?'

'I never—' She swallowed, nodded. 'Yes.'

'Then we'll work it out. We'll face it together. And whatever disappointments come our way, we'll face *them* together.' He drew her to his chest once more. 'That's what I want more than anything. No more running away, for either of us.'

Eleanor slipped her arms around Jace's waist, felt the warmth and strength of him and knew she had it—him—to lean on for now, for ever. The thought was amazing. Humbling too. 'No running away,' she repeated softly. She leaned back so she could look up at Jace and see the love and tenderness turn his eyes to soft grey. 'I love you, Jace. I'm sorry I panicked. I shouldn't have run away. I just couldn't think—'

'I know how that feels. But from now on we think. We talk. And we do it together.'

She nodded, unbelievably happy, incredibly grateful.

Jace turned back to the track that led to the villa. 'I'll have to ring the pilot and tell him the flight is cancelled.' He nodded to the house, glimmering with lights ahead. 'I'm afraid we have a good deal of explaining to do. My sisters are going to be seething with questions.'

'That's okay.'

There was a lot ahead, Eleanor knew. A lot to figure out

Work, children, family—even what continent they were going to live on. Yet as Jace led her back to his home she realised she wasn't afraid any more. She was excited. Whatever lay ahead, they would face it—together.

THE RELUCTANT DUKE
by Carole Mortimer

Forced to return to his family's seat, Lucan St Claire takes beautiful PA Lexie Hamilton with him. Lucan, however, has no idea that his new assistant isn't quite what she seems...

THE DEVIL WEARS KOLOVSKY
by Carol Marinelli

Swearing revenge on the Kolovskys, who abandoned him, Zakahr Belenki determines to destroy their fashion empire! Then he meets his secretary, Lavinia. Her honesty and passion for her job make Zakahr's conscience waver—and inflame his desire...

PRINCESS FROM THE PAST
by Caitlin Crews

Marriage to Prince Leo Di Marco was no fairytale, so Bethany Vassal ran away, hoping the man she loved would come and find her. Now the time has come for Leo to produce a royal heir—and Bethany must return to the castle whence she fled!

INTERVIEW WITH A PLAYBOY
by Kathryn Ross

Marco Lombardi *hates* journalists. Whisking reporter Isobel Keyes away in luxury seems like damage limitation—until she sparks his interest. Now Marco *wants* to kiss and tell...

On sale from 4th February 2011
Don't miss out!

Available at WHSmith, Tesco, ASDA, Eason and all good bookshops

www.millsandboon.co.uk

Walk on the Wild Side
by Natalie Anderson

Jack Greene has Kelsi throwing caution to the wind—it's hard to stay grounded with a man who turns your world upside down! Until they crash with a bump—of the baby kind...

Do Not Disturb
by Anna Cleary

A preacher's daughter, Miranda was led deliciously astray by wild Joe... Now the tables have turned—he's her CEO! But he's polished exterior doesn't disguise his devilish side...

Three Weddings and a Baby
by Fiona Harper

Jennie's groom vanished on their wedding night. When he returns, he has his *toddler* in tow! Jennie can't resist Alex's appeal and, for a successful businesswoman, one kid should be easy...right?

The Last Summer of Being Single
by Nina Harrington

Sebastien Castellano, prodigal city playboy, has mysteriously returned home to his sleepy French village. Now he's reminding single mum Ella how much fun the *single* part can be!

On sale from 4th February 2011
Don't miss out!

2 FREE BOOKS
AND A SURPRISE GIFT

We would like to take this opportunity to thank you for reading th
Mills & Boon® book by offering you the chance to take TWO mo
specially selected books from the Modern™ series absolutely FRE
We're also making this offer to introduce you to the benefits of th
Mills & Boon® Book Club™—

- **FREE home delivery**
- **FREE gifts and competitions**
- **FREE monthly Newsletter**
- **Exclusive Mills & Boon Book Club offers**
- **Books available before they're in the shops**

Accepting these FREE books and gift places you under no oblig
tion to buy, you may cancel at any time, even after receiving your fr
books. Simply complete your details below and return the entire pa
to the address below. You don't even need a stamp!

YES Please send me 2 free Modern books and a surprise gift.
understand that unless you hear from me, I will receive 4 superb ne
books every month for just £3.30 each, postage and packing free
am under no obligation to purchase any books and may cancel n
subscription at any time. The free books and gift will be mine to ke
in any case.

Ms/Mrs/Miss/Mr _____ Initials _____

Surname _____

Address _____

_____

_____ Postcode _____

E-mail _____

Send this whole page to: Mills & Boon Book Club, Free Book Offe
FREEPOST NAT 10298, Richmond, TW9 1BR

Offer valid in UK only and is not available to current Mills & Boon Book Club subscribers to this series
Overseas and Eire please write for details.. We reserve the right to refuse an application and applicants
must be aged 18 years or over. Only one application per household. Terms and prices subject to change
without notice. Offer expires 31st March 2011. As a result of this application, you may receive offers from
Harlequin Mills & Boon and other carefully selected companies. If you would prefer not to share in this
opportunity please write to The Data Manager, PO Box 676, Richmond, TW9 1WU.

Mills & Boon® is a registered trademark owned by Harlequin Mills & Boon Limited.
Modern™ is being used as a trademark. The Mills & Boon® Book Club™ is being used as a trademark.